Kingpin Killaz 3

Lock Down Publications and Ca$h Presents

Kingpin Killaz 3

A Novel by *Hood Rich*

Kingpin Killaz 3

Lock Down Publications
P.O. Box 870494
Mesquite, Tx 75187

Visit our website @
www.lockdownpublications.com

Copyright 2019 KINGPIN KILLAZ 3

Lock Down Publications
Like our page on Facebook: Lock Down Publications @
www.facebook.com/lockdownpublications.ldp
Cover design and layout by: **Dynasty Cover Me**
Book interior design by: **Shawn Walker**
Edited by: **Lauren Burton**

Hood Rich

Stay Connected with Us!

Submission Guideline.

Submit the first three chapters of your completed manuscript to ldpsubmissions@gmail.com, subject line: Your book's title. The manuscript must be in a .doc file and sent as an attachment. Document should be in Times New Roman, double spaced and in size 12 font. Also, provide your synopsis and full contact information. If sending multiple submissions, they must each be in a separate email.

Have a story but no way to send it electronically? You can still submit to LDP/Ca$h Presents. Send in the first three chapters, written or typed, of your completed manuscript to:

LDP: Submissions Dept
Po Box 870494
Mesquite, Tx 75187

DO NOT send original manuscript. Must be a duplicate.

Provide your synopsis and a cover letter containing your full contact information.

Thanks for considering LDP and Ca$h Presents.

Hood Rich

Chapter 1

Heinous

I opened the door and pushed it in, and the sight before me made my heart skip a beat. There, inside of the room, was Yani lying straight out on her stomach, her eyes closed tightly. She was naked from the waist up. The room smelled of musk and unwashed body.

I dropped the duffle bag of money to the floor and rushed to her side, kneeling beside her when I got there and pulling her into my arms, tapping her on the face. "Yani? Yani? Baby, wake up. Wake up."

I took two fingers and placed them to the side of her neck, checking for a pulse and finding a faint one after feeling around for a bit. Her head draped over my forearm, her mouth wide open. I turned my hand over and placed my skin close to her mouth to see if she was, in fact, breathing. After confirming she was, I tapped her face again. "Baby. Baby. Wake up."

A glance around the apartment told me everything I needed to know. There was a burnt spoon, along with an open package of aluminum foil. Inside of the foil was the heroin Yani had been nursing before I'd left her side. It looked almost half gone, which meant she'd done some serious partying while I'd been out. That worried me, along with the sight of her sprawled out on the hotel room floor.

Another slap to her cheek caused her to jerk a tad, frown, and very slowly open her eyes, blinking over and over. "Heinous?" She closed them again. "Is that you?"

I nodded as if she could see me. "Baby, get yo' ass up. We gotta get out of here. Come on." I pulled her wrist and made her sit up.

She groaned. "Oh, my fuckin' head is pounding. I need a wake-up baby. I need a wake-up right now or I'm going to be sick. Seriously, my head is spinning like a merry-go-round."

"A'ight, baby, we gon' get you right, but for right now I need you to get up so we can get out of here. We gotta leave this city right the fuck now." I pulled her to her feet. She staggered and crossed one ankle over the other before reaching out for me. She fell forward and into my awaiting arms.

"Heinous, I'm sick. I'm." She opened her mouth and threw up all over my shoulder, coughed, and threw up some more before falling to her knees and crying. More purging ensued.

I scrunched my nose and dared to look down at my arm. Her vomit coated it. The stench was almost too much for me. It made me gag. "What the fuck is wrong wit' you, girl?"

She shook her head. "I don't know. I just need a fix, Heinous. Please, give me a fix, and we can go anywhere you want to go." She wiped her mouth, crawled to the night table, and grabbed the aluminum foil package, opening it. Inside there was a rolled-up dollar bill I assumed she'd taped together. She took it, placed it inside of her right nostril, and tooted hard. She coughed, pulled on her nose, then did the same thing with the left one.

I stood looking down on her, feeling sick to my stomach. She was a monster I'd created. I'd been the one who had turned her out and onto the dangerous poison as a means of keeping her under my thumb. She'd threatened to leave me so many times, threaten to go her own separate way. After losing my mother, father, best friend, and sister, losing her would have been too much for me. So, in my mind, I'd done what was necessary.

8

She stood up and wiped her mouth. "A'ight, now I'm ready. I'm ready to embark on this journey with you, Heinous. Where are we going?" She stepped over the puddle of vomit as if it was no big thing.

"Yani, first of all, you gon' get yo' ass in the shower. You smell real bad, ma. Then we gon' bounce from this city and go down south and fuck wit' my cousin, Carti."

She nodded. "That's cool, Heinous. I think I met Carti before, right?" She yawned and headed toward the bathroom.

I followed her through the doors, ran the shower, and allowed some of the water to rinse her vomit from my arm. Then I was taking off my shirt and clothes. I watched her get naked. She reached and tested the temperature of the water before stepping inside and allowing the current to cascade all over her body. I stepped in behind her and grabbed the bottle of body wash. I squirted it into the palm of my hand and lathered her body with it. My hands roamed all over her naked body, soaping it up.

She laid her head back and moaned. "You didn't answer my question, baby. Haven't I met Carti before?"

I cupped her big breasts in the palms of my hands and smushed them together, placed my chin in the crux of her neck, and kissed the thick vein that ran along her left side. My piece pressed up against her ass cheeks. Yani was built, stacked with a small waist and a size-forty lowers. With her light caramel skin, hazel eyes, and natural hair, she was a physical force to be reckoned with. She'd been my woman on and off ever since high school. I had a crazy thing for her, and out of all the people I'd been close to while growing up, Yani was the last surviving party. I'd experienced one death after the next, and I knew it was just a matter of time before my clock ran out, which was why I wanted to get as far away from Chicago as possible.

Dallas sounded like the perfect escape. The destination had come to me on a whim. My cousin-in-law Carti and I were real cool. Though I hadn't seen her in person for a number of years, we'd managed to stay in contact by use of Snapchat, Facebook, and Instagram over the years. I didn't have any history in Dallas. It would be a fresh start for me and Yani. I had a bag full of the Prince of Mala Noche's money, and it was only a matter of time before he tracked me down and sent his goons at me full-fledge. We needed to bounce, and fast.

I pulled Yani's baby bottle-like nipples and sucked on her neck. "I think you did meet her, baby. I'm not sure. She came to the Chi a few times. A few years back was the latest. Whether you know her or not, we gon' be good, so don't trip." I humped forward into her booty, feeling my piece swell, and squeezed her big titties again.

"Mm, Heinous. That feel good, daddy. But wait, let me get everything clean first." She grabbed the loofah and began to wash under her arms and between her legs, taking her time to make sure she was doing a good job.

The shower continued to rain all over her. Her hair curled up and became thick, curly tresses. I kissed her neck and slid my hand down her stomach and into her crease. My fingers glided over her thick lips. I separated them and slid a digit inside of her hole, feeling her tunnel tighten around it. She spaced her feet and leaned back into me.

"Play wit' me, Heinous. Play wit' me like you always do. I need you to make me feel good." She rotated her cheeks in my lap.

My fingers were a blur going in and out of her, faster and faster. She closed her eyes tight and started to whimper. My dick got harder and harder.

"Ooh. Ooh. Heinous. Baby. Stop playing and fuck me. Fuck me real quick so we can go."

She bent over and placed her foot on the rim of the tub, reached back, and took ahold of my penis, searching for the opening to her pussy. As soon as she found it, I slammed forward, and grabbed her hips.

"Fuck! This pussy hot, baby. Gimme this shit."

She arched her back and placed her open palm on the wall, pushing back into my lap hard. "Mm, fuck me, Heinous. Fuck me. Fuck me harder. Mm. Mm. Mm. Grab my titties, too."

That was no problem. I took ahold of them and really got to hitting that pussy with no mercy, just like she liked it. Her thick thighs shook, along with her hefty ass cheeks. Her tongue traced her lips. Both nipples were sticking up from her mounds. Her hair fell over her face, concealing her from my view. She gasped and slapped the wall, pushing back into me as hard as she could. Her pussy felt like a tight, wet fist. It gripped and milked me, oozed all over my length. It felt like it got hotter with every stroke. I clenched my teeth as my eyes rolled into the back of my head, stroking deeper and faster, holding onto her big titties.

"Heinous. Heinous. Cum in me, daddy. Cum in me. Aw, fuck, I need to feel it so bad!"

She smashed back into me so hard I almost lost my footing. Then I grabbed her hips and held onto them for dear life, piping her like a monster until she screamed at the top of her lungs and came all over me.

The tugging of her inner walls became too much. Her wetness, her heat caused me to cum back-to-back in her channel before I fell against her, breathing hard.

***

I jumped on the highway an hour later, pushing the Ford Explorer to its limit while the El train screeched down the tracks in the middle of the expressway.

Yani reached over and cupped my piece, licked her lips, and smiled at me. "Daddy, on the real, the only thing I be needing for you to get me in line is some of that pipe. I mean, I'm still pissed at you for how shit went down with your mother, and a list of other things, but I am so happy to be leaving Chicago. I feel like we were living on borrowed time. I hope Dallas is so much different." She squeezed my dick and exhaled.

I nodded as I looked over to the big buildings decorating Chicago's skyline. I felt a bit emotional for having to leave the only city I'd ever really known. I'd put in a lot of blood, sweat, and tears, had lost a lot of my niggas, including my right-hand woman and my father, to the gun. The city had caused me a lot of pain, and I had made a whole mess of niggas feel my wrath as well. As much as I hated to leave, I knew it was in my best interest to do so. Not only did I have a bunch of enemies at my head, but there was also the law to think about. Because of me, one of the city's homicide detectives had been shanked, and I'd taken his bag of cash. Cash that belonged to the Mala Noche Cartel.

"Baby, I don't know what it's gon' be like in Dallas, but at least it's a fresh start. We got enough bread to do whatever we wanna do."

"Dang, that sound good. I know I wanna enroll in one of their universities. I want to get the best education I possibly can. That way we can leave this street shit behind and do everything the right way. Being in these streets ain't gon' do nothing but get us killed or locked up for the rest of our lives. I'm not ready to face either fate. I gotta get myself together so you can follow me." She snickered. "Following you gon' get us killed."

I looked her over and scoffed. "When we get down there, I'm finna sew shit up the right way. Bring that windy city shit to these country niggas. I got a few cousins in Dallas that's doing their thing, but they ain't really trapping like they should be. I got enough cash to break into that game down there and conquer that shit. Every misstep that I took in Chicago, I done learned from it. I know what I gotta do. But that shit you talking is obsolete. I been a boss, I just ain't have the chips to navigate the way I needed to. Now that I got 'em, it's over, trust me."

She rubbed all over my crotch and shook her head. "So we finna go to a whole other city and do the same dumb shit we did in Chicago? Is that what you telling me?" She let my piece go, sat back in her seat, and hugged her body. "I knew you wasn't gon' change. You ain't gon' stop until one of, or the both of us, is dead or somethin'. You're the smartest and dumbest nigga I know. Straight-up."

I mugged her li'l pretty ass. "Yani, shut up. You always got something slick to say. Maybe you should put this muthafucka in yo' mouth until I can figure out what we about to do when we get down there." I unzipped my pants, and pulled my dick out, stroked him up and down, and grabbed a handful of her hair. "Huh, bitch, straight-up."

She tried to pull her head back. "Stop playing wit' me, Heinous. Get your fingers out of my hair. You know I'm right, that's why you trying to shut me up," she snapped and hit at my hand.

"Handle this bidness, Yani. I ain't tryin' to talk about shit else. I need to have my mind right before I get down there. I been a street nigga my whole life. You knew what it was from the get-go. I gotta make shit happen for us. Always have, always will." I let her go.

She sat back in her seat and fixed her hair. "I can make it happen for myself. I ain't never been the type of female to depend on no nigga. You know how I get down. You insist on me following your ass. I'll make it with or without you, so don't get it twisted, Heinous." She curled her lip and scoffed. "Gotta be out if your fucking mind, trying to treat me less than a queen. Boy, I oughta slap some sense into you."

I laughed at that. She knew better than to raise her hand at me. For as long as we'd been fucking around, it had never gotten seriously violent between us, but if ever she tried to take it there, I would have to put her in her place real fast and with no hesitation. "Yani, I don't know what's going through your brain, but you know better than to try that physical shit wit' me. I never wanna put my hands on you, but if you –"

"*But if I* nothin'. If you don't want to put your hands on me, then don't. It's as simple as that. However, if you ever decide to get down on me like that, well, just know it ain't sweet. I'ma fight your ass back until I can't anymore. Then, if you do mess me up too bad, you better watch your back every second of every day, because you're suppose to have more respect for me than that." She looked out of the window. "Still can't believe we're leaving Chicago, though. I thought we'd be stuck in that ratchet-ass city forever."

I gazed upon the skyline again and felt a sense of despair come over me. Soon Chicago would be nothing more than a distant, painful memory. "Yeah, I can't, either. But what better way to leave the city behind than you hitting daddy off for old times' sake. You already know ain't nobody got they head on their shoulders like you do, Yani."

"Shut up." She slapped my thigh and took ahold of my piece, squeezing him, then slowly stroking him in her little fist. "Daddy, you so damn freaky. All you think about is sex all day long." She licked her lips, undid her seatbelt, and kneeled on her seat, leaning over the center console by my right thigh. She kissed my head, then sucked me into her mouth.

In less than thirty seconds she was spearing her head so fast I was shamefully on the verge of cumming, even though I was trying to hold back. The noises were driving me crazy. Her pretty eyes were closed tight. Her jaw hollowed in and out as she did her thing.

I sat back and did the best I could to concentrate on the road ahead of me. Watching the El train go past on the track, I started to think to myself that it might have been the last time I'd be able to see the train again in person. I felt remorseful, a bit sick, but at the same time relieved. Relieved because I'd be getting a fresh start at a new place with new people. I looked forward to crushing Dallas, to turning the city upside down, to bringing a slice of Chicago to the south.

Yani tightened her hold on my dick, then removed it altogether, slurping me hands-free. The heat from her mouth became intense. "Mm. Mm." More slurping. Faster sucking.

I stared to rise from the seat, humping into her mouth. My fingers gripped the steering wheel. My foot stepped on the gas before I removed it altogether. More humping. "Shit. Shit. Ma!" I slammed upward into her mouth, then I was cumming back-to-back while she swallowed and used her fist to pump all of my cream out of me.

She removed her head and licked all over the helmet. "Mm, there you go, daddy. Now, tell Chicago to kiss both of our asses."

She got back in the passenger seat and replaced her seatbelt. "Heinous, I swear to God, if we get down here and you get to acting all funny, I'm bouncing on yo' ass. I got me a nice li'l stash that's within reach, so if the going gets tough, I'ma get ghost. Know that." She ran her fingers through her hair. "I need a fix. My head starting to hurt real bad." She grabbed her Gucci purse off of the floor beside her, then rummaged around inside of it, looking for her work. After not finding it, her eyes got bucked, and she looked depressed. "Heinous, we gotta go back to the hotel. Seriously. I left all of that work in my other bag in the closet."

I shrugged my shoulders. "That's fucked up. You about to be real sick then, 'cause I only got a li'l product left for me." I meant that, too. I knew we had a nice drive to go. I was gon' take a few toots every so often so I could conserve the li'l bit of boy I had left. I knew when I made it to Dallas I would be able to cop some more, but as it stood, I had less than three grams, which was really nothing.

Yani smacked her lips and frowned. "Dang, you gon' do me like that? You gon' act funny knowing I'm about to be sick? Really?" She shook her head.

"Man, why don't you take yo' irritating-ass to sleep? You giving me a fuckin' headache. Maybe by the time you wake up we'll be closer to our destination." I tucked my piece back in and zipped my jeans.

She scoffed. "Heinous, I'm feeling sick. Now, is you gon' get me right or not? Seriously. I'm about to freak out over here." She stared to rummage through her purse again in a mock attempt to find the product she'd placed in her other bag.

"Shorty, if I give you a bit to ease yo' sick, will you lay yo' ass back and just shut up? Like I told you before, I need to collect my thoughts before we get down there, and you're filling in every moment of silence with some bullshit. So, before I give you a few crumbs, you gotta let me know what's good."

She grumbled, "Yeah, man, damn. Let me just get a taste, and I'll fall back. If you don't wanna do that, we can make a pit stop at the next exit. Halstead is coming up. I know a few places where I can get some A-1 dog food that'll keep me laced. It's your call."

I stepped on the gas and switched lanes, then dug into my boxer briefs and pulled out the sandwich bag of aluminum foil packages. I took a dime and gave it to her. "Huh, shorty, that's yours. Now, do it and fall back. We got a long journey ahead."

She smiled. "Thank you, daddy. I promise I ain't gon' mess wit' you for at least four hours."

I laughed. "Yeah, I'ma hold you to it."

Hood Rich

Chapter 2

When I pulled up in front of Carti's two-story, red brick home the next day, it was bright and sunny at twelve in the afternoon. She was already sitting on the porch with two other females. Before I could throw my whip in park all the way, she was breaking her neck to get down the stairs. Once she made it to the sidewalk, she ran around the front of the truck and pulled my door open.

"Heinous, get yo' ass out here, playboy, and give me my hug. I been waiting on you to show up since yesterday."

Carti was light-skinned with electric green eyes and about five feet, five inches tall. Her hair was naturally long and straightened with subtle burgundy highlights that made her yellow complexion pop. She was my mother's brother's wife's daughter, which made her my cousin-in-law. Throughout the years we'd developed a strong bond. My cousin had swag, and I dug her style on so many levels. At the age of twenty-five, she we already the owner of her own beauty shop and strip club. She was about her chips.

I removed the seatbelt and stepped out. Before we'd gotten to her place, I'd stopped at the mall so I could get fresh. I'd gotten my hair cut, and I was rocking a black-and-purple Gucci fit with the red-bottomed, matching purple-and-black retro Jordans. I had two diamond studs in each earlobe and a nice gold link around my neck that coincided with my gold Movado watch. My cologne was also Gucci for men.

She ran into my arms and laid her head on my chest, hugging me tight. "Damn, I missed you. You smell so good."

I held her and kissed her cheek. She was fitted in a simple Fendi sundress, yellow and blue. Her sandals were Fendi as well. "Yeah, cuz. Long time, no see. But it's good. I'm here now. How you been?"

She stepped out of my embrace and looked past me and into the truck. "Hello, you must be Yani?"

Yani waved. "Yeah, how are you doing? Thank you for allowing us to stay with you for a spell, or until we find our own place. That was real nice of you."

Carti smiled. "That's no problem. Damn, Heinous, she fine as hell. I ain't know yo' bitch was gon' be this bad. Say, Yani, do you fuck wit' females, too, or are you one of them straight-laced, boring Chicago bitches?"

Yani jerked her head back. "First of all, I ain't nobody's bitch. I'm a queen. Secondly, I only fuck wit' bad bitches. So, you do the math."

Carti nodded and sucked her bottom lip. "Well, excuse me. Mm. I like her, Heinous. Not only is she fine as hell, but she jazzy as a muthafucka. That'll get you a long way in Dallas. Straight-up. Do you strip, or would you be interested in making a few grand a night if I could give you a spot in a money-making club that caters to women as bad as you? If that is somethin' you would consider, then we can work on changing your life this weekend."

"Man, calm down, Carti, damn. Give my baby enough time to step foot on the concrete of Dallas. Yo' li'l ass going so hard already."

Yani snickered. "Damn, and to think the south is supposed to be way slower than us back home." She shook her head. "I see I'ma have to watch myself down here, huh?"

Carti shook her head. "Nall, baby, you just gotta watch out for boss bitches down here. If a ho see you as a threat, she gon' find a way to get you under her thumb so she can capitalize off of the strengths she sees in you. The first thing that screamed to me was your beauty. You can make a lot of money down here, which is why I wanna be the one to put you on. I got the connects and the club to showcase your beauty. I can't wait to see what you look like when you step out of the truck. I can already tell you're strapped, though."

I put my arm around her neck and kissed her cheek. "You about that money, cuz. That's why I come down here to fuck wit' you. Chicago burnt up. I need a fresh start, just like I told you about on the phone. I need for us to sit back and get an understanding. I want to get to eating ASAP, and so do my lady."

Carti nodded. "Yeah, well, you already know I'ma get you right. You been through a lot. You in my city now, so let's get it." She waved to Yani. "Come on, love. I done cooked a nice lunch for y'all, and dinner is almost done as well. I started on it yesterday, and I'll wrap it up tonight. Know I gotta show my ass. This that 'Southern Hospitality.' Come on."

Yani stepped out of the truck in her black-and-pink, body-hugging Prada skirt-dress. She had pink lemonade diamonds in her ear and was rocking the matching Hermes bag over lemon red-bottoms. She slid her Chanel sunglasses over her eyes while her curly hair blew in the gentle breeze. She looked so good that I wanted to bend her li'l thick-ass over and smash her in front of Carti and her crew. It was like I was seeing her for the first time.

"It feel good out here." She came over and took ahold of my hand.

When we got onto the porch, there were two dark-skinned females sitting there. They stood up in some of the tiniest skirts I had ever seen. Both sets of chocolate thighs were shining in the light. They looked as if they had been heavily coated with baby oil. They wore cut-off tank tops that showcased their flat stomachs. Both had piercings in their navels.

"These my li'l kittens, right here, cuz. This is Africa, and this is Sudan. They're twins, and'll ride to the dirt for me. Ain't that right, babies?" Carti asked, slipping her arms below their waists and holding them.

Africa smiled, laugh lines emphasizing her caramel contact lenses. "To the dirt, mama. You already know what it is." She licked her juicy lips. "I do hope we get to play wit' him, though. Wardy, look good enough to eat."

"I'll second that motion," Sudan added, looking me up and down hungrily. She came over and hugged me, kissed my neck, then backed up. "It's a pleasure to meet you, Heinous. We heard you one of them roughneck niggas that had them city boys running for their lives. That's what's up, Wardy. I like them real thugs."

Her lips were layered with heavy lip gloss. They were pink and looked like candy. Just looking at them had me feeling some type of way.

Yani stepped in front of her and hugged up on me. "Look, first thing you hoez need to know is I'll kill a bitch over this nigga. Me and him been through it all together, so if it comes down to it, he gon' help me bury your body somewhere it can't be found. Y'all need to back up until we get to know what's good down here. Chicago in the building. Straight-up."

The twin backed away and held up heir hands at shoulder level. "Okay," they muttered in unison.

I laughed and placed my arm around both Carti and Yani. "Yo, I'm starving like a muthafucka. Let's go in here and get some of this grub, baby. Calm down."

"Yeah, let's do that. Then we gotta re-up, Heinous. You know what I'm talking about. I'm starting to feel some type of way." She shivered and held me tighter.

"I'm on it, boo. Let's eat, and that's next on the agenda."

***

After lunch, Yani decided to settle into the guest room while me and Carti grabbed a bottle of Hennessy, a box of cigarillos, and an ounce of Dallas Loud and headed to the den so we could talk business. She waited until I walked past her before she closed the door behind me. She sat across from me on the love seat while I plopped onto her white leather couch. The den was a relatively good size. The carpet was all white, there was a big projector screen that could roll down from the ceiling, an entertainment system, and a piano. It smelled like fresh Febreeze.

Carti got to stuffing one of the cigars. "Yo, so I know what you used to be on back in the Windy, but you're in Dallas now. What's on your mind?"

She handed me a blunt and I took it, even though I was craving that boy. My stomach felt like it was in knots. I needed a fix soon. I had about a sixteenth left, and I was nursing it. I'd tooted a pinch before I came to the den with Carti, and it helped to take some of the sickness away. But Yani was right: we needed to get more of it soon or we were going to be in for it. I didn't know how to propose that to Carti, and I didn't know if I felt comfortable letting her know me and Yani had a problem. I needed to feel her out a bit more.

"Cuz, you already know how I get down. I'm trying to get my feet wet down here right away. I got a few chips stacked away that I eventually wanna do somethin' long-term and positive with, but for now I wanna snatch my portion of the slums. I'm a hood nigga. Always have been."

She took a long pull from her blunt and inhaled the smoke, then held it while nodding her head. "What kind of chips you talking about? Because if it's enough, then it's best you jump into this real estate thing with me. I just found a new hot spot of real estate where the apartment buildings are goin' for the low. The buildings will need a little tender love and care, but after the investment we'll be able to make five times the amount of money we initially invested into them in about two years' time. There are also some businesses that are going under that need investors. I can use a partner in this second strip club I'm about to open in six months. I mean, there are all kinds of positive things you can jump into. You ain't gotta necessarily jump into the game down here. You can go a whole different route and be filthy rich in no time."

"That sound cool, but I still wanna know what these slums be about. I ain't college-smart like that, to be running businesses and shit. I mean, I can handle the basics, but as far as real estate and all that shit go, I'ma need some serious education for all of that. And that take time. And time is money. Money is all I care about. You feel?"

"I most definitely do. A'ight then, if you insist on fucking wit' the game, then you might as well wait until Crescent get back in town this weekend. That nigga is the heart of the slums. If anything going down in Dallas, he got his hands in it. You talking about plugs, then that's definitely the way to go." She took another pull. "I really wish you'd fuck wit' me on this positive shit, though, especially if you saying you got some chips stacked up. It's to the point that as long as it's a few hunnit bands, nigga, I can take that, add it with what I got, and we can make some major moves. Give Uncle Sam his due and still be paid in full. But old habits die hard."

There was a knock on the door. Yani twisted the knob and stuck her head in the room. "Daddy, where is your suitcase with the paper in it?" She gave me a look to let me know *paper* meant serious cash. "I don't see it."

"Baby, it's in the truck, behind the back seat, right where I left it. Matter fact, go grab it and bring it in the house," I ordered her. In my haste to get into Carti's house, I'd neglected to grab it, which had been extremely negligent of me.

"Oh, I ain't check back there. My bad for disturbing y'all. I'll go." She pressed her lips to her hand and blew the kiss to me before closing the door.

Carti stared at me, then snickered. "Damn, ol' girl seem like she gon' be all over yo' ass. The worst thing you could have done is brought a bitch wit' you down to the south. You 'bout to run into so many hoez that's gon' wanna fuck you just because you from Chicago and you got a nice amount of bread. Yani gon' wind up getting her feelings hurt. I hope you know that, and you're cool with it." She crossed her thick thighs. The sundress rose and revealed her skin underneath.

"She good. I been fuckin' wit' shorty for a long time. She know how to get in where she fit in. But back to cuz, though, you think he got a plug on that China, or even some of that tar baby?" I really ain't wanna talk this kind of bidness with her, but I was getting anxious. I had to get my hands on a nice amount of boy before both Yani and myself lost our minds.

Carti shot me a devilish look. "Cuz, what you know about that dog food? You getting your nose dirty?"

I adjusted on the couch uncomfortably. "A li'l bit. It ain't no major thing right now, but me and my bitch fuckin' wit' it on some recreational shit. Why, you got a plug?"

She bit into her lip. "I mights. It just depends on how much you talking? I get down a little bit myself, but I don't want my hoez knowing that. The people that work under you should never know what your weaknesses are. Nine times out if ten they'll try to use it against you at a later date. I can't have none of that happening. I got some shit thata blow your mind, though. Let me put his bullshit out. Weed don't do shit for me no more." She stood up and pulled her dress down. "I'll be right back with some of that good-good." She got to the door and twisted the knob.

I was so happy at what she'd just said that I could barely think straight. My stomach did a series of flips. My face flushed, and my throat got tight. I felt uneasy, excited, and thirsty for the drug. I needed it.

"Uh, Heinous, I hope you know I plan on getting some of that dick. We ain't kids no more. We old enough to fuck now, and I'm tryna see what that pipe game be about. You see this?" She lifted her dress all the way up to expose the yellow satin panties underneath. Her cleft was so fat the material had sunk in between the lips. She rubbed her finger up and down it, pushed it further into herself. "This pussy grown now. All that playing around we used to do as curious kids, I'm ready now, so don't let yo' bitch prevent you from getting some of this." She pulled the crotch band aside and flashed her naked pussy. It looked swollen and meaty. Her fingers glided through it before she pulled her panties back in place.

There was a loud banging on the door, then I heard Yani's voice. "Daddy. Daddy. Somebody just stole your truck from in front of the house!" she hollered.

I jumped off of the couch and dropped the blunt on the floor, pulled Carti out of the way, and opened the door. "Baby, what are you talking about?" My heart began to pound in my chest. I grabbed her by the shoulders firmly.

"Baby, when I went back outside after taking the first few suitcase upstairs, I came back downstairs to find somebody jumping in the driver's seat of the truck. Before I could get on the porch good, they were storming away from the curb with the rest of our stuff in it. All of the clothes you just bought us, and the suitcases of money." At saying the last part, she lowered her voice.

"What!" I threw her li'l ass out of my way and rushed outside. The sun was shining bright. It felt hot and humid. There were houses up and down the block. A few of the porches were filled with people. When I came storming out of the house, all eyes were on me. I rushed down the steps and to the space where my truck had been parked. Disbelieving. I didn't know how much money I had lost, how much was in the truck because I had never sat down and counted it. All I knew was that I felt sick, like I had pneumonia.

Yani came down the steps and rubbed my back. "Baby, are you okay? Huh?"

I felt like the sun was trying to burn a hole through the top of my waves. I started to get more and more angry. Lowering my head, I tried to calm down. "Yani, did you have the door open while you was moving our shit?"

"Yeah, but I was going as fast as I could. I mean, I didn't think nobody would try and steal the truck with all of these people sitting on their porches. So, wait, you're trying to say it's my fault?" She touched her chest.

"Man, we had a bunch of new clothes in the back seat. Suitcases and all of that shit. You was raised in Chicago. You know how muthafuckas get down. You been here less than three hours, and already you acting brand new as fuck. Hell yeah, I'm blaming you. Ain't nobody tell you to start moving this shit yet. I thought you was upstairs lying down. Fuck!" I covered my face with my hands and looked down the street both ways. Whoever had stolen the truck had gotten away with at least three hundred thousand in cash, but for all I knew it could have been more than that. I suddenly felt dizzy.

I took my hands away and glared at the people who were sitting on their porches and made my way over to them. There were four bigger girls sitting on the porch, fanning themselves. The closer I got, the more they began to smile. I approached the one who was sitting on the bottom step. She had a newspaper folded up and was waving it in front of her face. Sweat slid down the side of her cheek. She was fitted in a colorful dress that was as bright as the sun. "Uh, excuse me, sweetheart, but were you able to see who stole my truck while my friend was unloading it?" I made a point to call Yani my friend just so this chubby broad could think she had a shot wit' me. She was a bit of a cutie, too, but coming up with her was the furthest thing from my mind. I was a long way from home, and if I couldn't track down my cash, I was about to be in a fucked up position.

She stopped fanning herself, and looked back at the other big girls. They smiled at her before she turned back to me. "Yeah, I think I seen who stole yo' shit, Wardy, but that ain't my bidness. Besides, you got them Illinois plates on thur, anyway. You made yourself a target." She started to fan herself again, this time with her eyes closed.

I scrunched my face and had a vision of choking her ass out. I couldn't believe this bitch. I was wondering what happened to the southern hospitality. "So, because I'm from out if town, it's okay for somebody to steal my shit when I go to unloading my things?"

"Seems that way, playboy. That's what happened, ain't it?" she snickered. "Welcome to Dallas."

Yani must've been listening from a distance. She stormed over and bumped me slightly out of the way. "Uh, I don't know who you think you are or if you think it's cool to laugh at other people's misfortunes, but it ain't. Bitch, I don't see shit funny, and it ain't sweet just 'cause we from Illinois. Shit'll get sour around this muthafucka real fast, trust me. Now, you said you know who stole our shit. Bitch who did it?"

The big sista stood up and dropped her homemade fan to the concrete. "Say, Wardy, who the fuck you thank you talkin' to? You a long way from home."

Yani balled up her fists and took her earrings out of her earlobes. "Bitch, you gon' tell me who stole my nigga shit, or on everythang I love, I'm about to see what yo' blood look like. Now, try me." She handed me her diamond earrings.

The other big girls stood up on the porch, and acted like they were about to assist their comrade. They all looked alike, so they may have been sisters. One of them, who was the shortest and I assumed the youngest, balled her fist and slammed it into the palm of her hand. "I'll handle that li'l skinny bitch, sis. Watch out." She made her way down the steps, taking her earrings off like Yani had.

Before she got off of the last step, Yani rushed her, swinging haymakers. The first blow caught the girl right in the nose, splattering it. The second blow was to her chin, and the third was a kick to her chest, knocking her backward on the stairs. She groaned loudly and curled into a ball.

"Bitch! Now, who the fuck stole my nigga shit? If I gotta whip all of you hoez to get the answer, then so be it." She hauled off and smacked the shit out if the first big girl who had done a bunch of laughing, catching her off guard. "Bitch, especially you!"

The big girl held her face and jogged up the stairs. "Kills stole yo' truck. Damn! That shit ain't got nothing to do wit' us. Take that crazy bitch back across the street wit' you and leave us alone."

Yani stepped onto the first step. "Bitch, who is Kills? Where that nigga stay? We need that address right now. He got our shit, and until we get it back, I'ma whoop one of you bitches every single day. That's on my grandmother."

The first big girl with the colorful dress held her face. "He stay eight blocks over on Chambers. A green house. It usually got a bunch of niggas in front of it. Take that drama to his doorstep, not ours. This shit ain't fair. Carti, come and get yo' people before I call the police!" she screamed.

Yani rushed up the steps, and the big girls tried their best to run into the house one after the other, but not before she was able to take ahold of a different sister. She grabbed her by her hair and slung her backward. She crashed to the porch, and Yani dragged her down the steps and to the concrete.

"Stop! Stop! Leave my li'l sister alone!" the first chick yelled.

"Nall, fuck that. Where Killa stay? Bitch, you 'bout to show me right now. Come on." She helped her to her feet and grabbed her by the neck.

"He crazy! If he find out I told you where he stay at, he gon' try and do something to us. Please, leave me and my sisters out of this. I'm begging you," she whimpered with her head yanked backward.

Carti ran across the street with her iPhone XS in her hand. "Cuz, let that bitch go. I know where he stay and some of the niggas he be wit'. We don't need to involve them." Carti stopped in the middle of the street and started to text somebody on her phone. The sun shined off of her forehead, causing it to look greasy. After sending the text, she looked up at Yani.

Yani had her arm around the chubby girl's throat. She tightened it, choking her. "Bitch, the next time you see

30

somebody taking advantage of a vulnerable person, you either say something to prevent it or you and your sisters keep y'all mouths closed. Everything ain't always funny. Y'all don't know what we had in that truck.' She slung her to the ground and kicked her in the ass. "Get up Bitch. Tell yo big sister she betta hope we get our shit back, or that's her ass." She walked over to me with her chest heaving up and down, frowning.

I moved her hair out if her face. "Baby, chill, you good. Dem bitches know the Chi on deck now. You did ya thing. Now, calm down. I'll take it from here. Where these fuck-niggas at?" I asked Carti.

Carti waved for us to follow her, walking across the street toward her lemon Lexus truck sitting on 28-inch gold Pirellis. Her dress hugged her ass as the wind blew, molding the moons. She opened her driver's door, and spoke over the top of the hood at me. "Heinous you get in the back and let Yani get in the front. I don't even want these niggas to see your face until the time is right for you to holler at them, which a probably be when Crescent get back. Come on let's roll." She popped the locks.

I got into the back as ordered, and Yani took the passenger's seat. I felt naked. I ain't have no pistol on me, or nothing to defend myself. I felt vulnerable and mad at the same time. I was ready to smoke something over my scratch. I didn't give a fuck where we was or how long we'd been in the city. I had visions of turning this bitch upside down for my cash. I was still unsure of just how much it was. All I knew was it was more than I was willing to lose.

I closed the door, and Carti's tints came into play. She turned around in her seat and eyed me closely. "Look, Heinous, this nigga Killa is plugged with hem uptown niggas over on McKinney Avenue. They get all about jacking and drive-bys. They originally came from California. They only been down this way for about five years now. The five years they been down here, they been terrorizing the city. I say that to say that if Killa is really the one who stole your truck and stole your money – wait, about how much is it, again?"

I flared my nostrils. "I don't even know. I ain't have a chance to count it. But it's way more than I'm willing to lose. That's all you need to know."

"So, you talking hunnits of thousands, then?" she asked.

I nodded. "Hunnits on hunnits."

She blew air out of her jaw. "Fuck, that's gon' be a problem. All they do is buy guns and blow. If they came up on that kind of money, I can see Killa an' 'em taking their crew to the next level. Damn, Crescent ain't like getting this news. He hate Killa. He used to be his right-hand man back in the day when they were hitting licks over in Houston, robbing dope boys. But when Crescent wound up coming upon a lick that grossed him one point five million, he turned legit, and Killa didn't like that. They became rivals and been at odds ever since."

"Carti, fuck this nigga's history. If he got my paper, then I'm smoking him and taking my shit back. I won't give a fuck how many niggas he plugged with or who he is. Don't nobody take shit from me and get away with it. This city ain't seen a killer until they saw me. Trust that. Now, let's roll. Fuck the warning and precautions."

She was quiet for a second, looking me over, then turned around. "Okay, but here." She reached under her driver's seat and handed me a chrome, thirteen-shot nine-millimeter. "Just in case shit get out of hand. I know you gon' make sure we straight as long as you got one of these."

I cocked it, popped out the clip to make sure it was loaded, then slammed the magazine back into it. "Now we talking. Let's roll to McKinney. Let me see what's really good."

Hood Rich

Chapter 3

Carti's truck eased onto the crowded block of McKinney Avenue. All of the porches appeared to have somebody sitting on them. The street was narrow, and the houses looked run down and old.

We drove past a vacant lot that had about twenty or more dudes grouped up inside of it. They had bright yellow bandanas hanging out of their back pockets. I ain't know what it meant, and I didn't care, either. Most of them were wearing tight wife-beaters and fitted caps turned to the back. They looked like they'd been pumping iron all day long, with the exception of a few skinny ones who looked like all they did was smoke dope all day long.

"Which one of them niggas is Killa?" I asked with my forehead against her back tinted window. I wanted to get a make on him so I could see who I was dealing with. After being in the game for so long, I was able to see a nigga, size him up, and be able to tell if he was about that life or not just from his mannerisms. I was thirsty to see Killa, especially since he had a name like that.

Carti rubbernecked as she slowed the truck. "I don't see him, but that's definitely his guys, though. They look like they up to something. Why are they all mounted up like that?"

I lowered the window and got ready to stick the nose of my gun out of it so I could get to busting. "Man, I don't know, but if these his niggas, then I might as well knock off as many of them as I can right now. Save myself some time and energy later. You sho that's his guys?"

Carti stepped on the gas and pulled off of the block. She turned the corner with a mug on her face. "Heinous, I know you wasn't about to buck at them niggas from the back seat of my truck, was you?"

I stayed silent and slid the nose of the nine back into my waistband. I ain't wanna lie to her. Had she stayed there for five more seconds, I was about to knock off as many of them yellow flag-carrying niggas as I could. I figured Killa would find a way to use them to his advantage later, so it would be in my best interest to trim the fat.

My silence must've gotten to her. She smacked her lips and shook her head. "Dang, Heinous. You gon' have all of our asses in jail, and down here in Texas they lock you up and throw away the key. This ain't Chicago, nigga. These southerners ain't got no problem losing yo' ass. You gotta be smarter down here, if not for your sake, then for mine and your lady's."

Yani scoffed. "They ain't got no bidness stealing my nigga's truck and money. They gon' bring this wrath onto themselves. I get what you're saying about being smart, but for as long as I've known Heinous, he ain't never took no loss lying down. Dallas about to be fucked over. I know that for a fact."

I didn't know if it was the heroin that had turned Yani into an instant savage or if all of the deaths we'd experienced had, but whatever the case, I was falling for her more and more by the hour because that G-shit was coming out of her. That thoroughbred Chicago shit that had been in me ever since I was a youngin' running through the streets of the Chi, busting my gun wit' no remorse. My whole life I'd always wanted a rider like that. A female version of me. Brat had come close, but she'd wound up crossing me somethin' nasty in the end, and I had to let justice take its course with her.

"Carti, you're right. I wasn't thinking. I just don't like a muthafucka hitting me for nothing. I feel like a li'l bitch right now. Like I done came down here and these country niggas done fucked me wit' no Vaseline." I meant every word of what I'd just said, too.

"Nall, don't feel like that, cuz. Ain't nobody fuck you like nothing. That nigga Killa stole your truck because the doors were open. It ain't like he took you out of it. That would be a whole other story. And as far as the loot he came upon, that was pure luck. I'ma make sure you get his ass, trust me. Crescent'll be back in a few days, and I already know once he find out what took place he gon' flip his top. It's gallons of bad blood between them niggas. You just gotta be patient." She rolled back to her house and pulled her truck in her garage before getting out of it. "Y'all come on in the house and calm down." She headed inside.

I got ready to get out of the truck when Yani grabbed my shoulder. "Wait, Heinous, are you seriously mad at me about this? You know I would have never allows for this to happen if I could've prevented it."

"I ain't sweating that shit, Yani. You made a mistake, and so did I. I should have brought all of the bags inside of the house first, then went and sat down with Carti. I think it's this dope, though. It's throwing me off. It's fucking wit' my head. But at the same time, I ain't about to let these country niggas enjoy the fruits of my labor. I'ma try and wait for my cousin to get back, then go at them full-fledge. I gotta have my money. We can't do shit without it."

"I got about two thousand put up. If you need that to move and groove, you can get fifteen hundred of it. Baby, when do you think we gon' get some more product? I feel like if we had a taste, then we'd be able to figure out how to proceed. I mean, have you even talked to Carti about that yet?" She scratched the side of her neck, and then rubbed the spot, licked her lips, and avoided making eye contact with me.

"She got something for us right now. She say it's good, too. I'ma find out who her connect is, and if it's as good as she say it is, then I'ma hit his ass so we'll be right for a nice amount of time. I ain't with this fien'in shit. I feel like a hype or somethin'."

She nodded her head. "Me too. I'll never forgive you for putting this shit in my system, Heinous. You turned me into what I am, and to be honest with you, that sniffing shit don't work for me. I need it here." She pointed to the vein I'd previously injected the poison into her through. I could see a few track marks along it. Track marks that made my stomach turn upside down. I still couldn't believe I had to go that route just to keep her with me. I would never forgive myself.

"Baby, I'm sorry, but I'm fucked up, too. I need that shit the same way. I been trying to put it up here," I pointed to my nose, "but it don't last as long, and it barely does anything for me. I should have never brought you on board, but I couldn't have you leaving me when I needed you the most. You're my heart, Yani. You know that."

She lowered her head. "Yeah, but this still isn't fair. I didn't want this habit. I don't think I'm strong enough to sustain it. All I think about is boy, all day, all night. My body calls out for it, and so does my soul. What do we do when the yearnings get so bad that we need it every second of every day, Heinous? What do we do if we turn into your mother?"

"I don't know, baby. We just gotta fight and not allow for that shit to happen. That's all. We're in this together. I apologize for hooking you, but I can't stand to not have you by my side. I just can't. We been through it all together. You're my heart."

"You're mine, too. That's the only reason I ain't killed your ass for what you did to me. Trust and believe that it's crossed my mind, but because you're you, I just let it roll off my shoulders. But I love you, Heinous, and we gon' get that fuck-nigga Killa. I'm riding wit' you through it all. That's on my grandmother."

I nodded. "I know, Boo, and I'm riding wit' you, too. We gon' turn this bitch upside down real soon. That's my word."

***

Later that night, Carti hit me wit' a zip of some China she'd gotten from one of her connects as I was coming out of the upstairs bathroom. "Here, Heinous. This should help you and yo' bitch take the edge off for a li'l while. I just got off of Snapchat wit' Crescent and told him what was good wit' that nigga Killa. He say he'll be back in town tomorrow night, considering the circumstances. He sounded real pissed. You already know he always had a place in his cold heart for you. So that's what's good. Fall back for the night, and don't forget what I said about this." She cupped my dick and squeezed it. "I been wondering what this pipe feel like ever since I was eleven years old. You remember all of that freaky shit we used to do? Playin' wit' and sucking all on each other? Don't you?" She kissed my neck, then licked along it, sucked my earlobe into her mouth, and purred.

My dick started to get real hard in her grasp. A few of the flashbacks from when we were kids played over in my mind. Her bald kitty, and how she used to like when I licked up and down it while she moaned into the pillows. Our parents would be in the next room, none the wiser. Every time she came over, they'd always have us go into my room so we could play, and in less than five minutes I'd have my hands up her dress, playin' wit' her li'l kitty while she backed up against the wall and begged for me to stop, knowing damn well she didn't want me to. I'd get her nice and wet before getting on my knees and eating her out while she held her dress up, like I'd watched the dudes do in the porno DVDs my father kept tucked in the closet of his den. She'd hold my head and shake like crazy as she came, humping into my mouth, then we'd switch places. Those were some of the best times of my young life. "Yeah, I remember. How could I ever forget?"

She slipped her hand into my waistband, then all the way down until she was touching the hot skin of my piece. She stepped forward and moaned. "Damn, it done got real big now. I need some of that. I'ma fuck wit' you later, though." She kissed my cheek and walked off with her purple biker shorts all up inside of her fat booty. With each step she took, it jiggled. My piece throbbed like crazy.

Sudan stepped into the hallway and shook her head. "Damn, I see y'all real freaky around this place. Don't think I ain't just see what you and your 'cousin' did." She did air quotes to emphasize her point, snickered, and walked past me, heading downstairs and singing an Ella Mai song under her breath.

I wanted to holler that Carti was only my cousin by law, but thought 'fuck it.' Sudan was a nobody to me. I didn't care what she thought. From as far as I could see, she ain't have nothing going for herself other than stripping, and she worked in Carti's club, which meant Carti was the boss of her.

I shrugged my shoulders and pushed open the door of the guest bedroom me and Yani was staying in. As soon as I did, she hopped off the bed and ran right past me into the bathroom and closed the door. I could hear her throwing up.

Minutes later, she flushed the toilet and was swishing mouthwash around inside of her mouth. She stuck her head in the room, then disappeared, sucking in cool air. "Heinous, I'm sick. We gotta get right. I'm willing to go out and cop some by myself rather than keep dealing with this sickness. Seriously, I'm cramping and all kind of shit. What Carti talking about?" She sat on the edge of the bed and looked sick. There were light bags under her eyes. Her face looks flushed, and she looked as if she'd lost a nice bit of weight. Her face was still real beautiful, but it also appeared more boney and sunken.

I turned my back to her and opened the aluminum foil Carti had given me. The China was thick and grainy with a slight twinkle to it. I took a pinch and sprinkled it back into the pile. I could feel the pores of my fingers absorbing it. They tingled, which caused me to become excited. "She say Crescent'll be back tomorrow night, and we gon' go holler at that Killa nigga. In the meantime, she gave me this li'l treat to tide us over. This shit look good, too."

Yani stood up and peeked over my shoulder. "Dang, what you hiding it for? I know I'm about to get me some of that." She rolled up the sleeve on her blouse, went to the dresser, and pulled out our works. She sat down on the other side of the bed and got everything ready.

I handed her a nice amount for her to cook up and sterilize. In a matter of minutes she was drawing the poison through the rug and into the syringe. She shook during the process. I could tell she was overly excited, and I was getting there myself.

"So, who gon' go first, Heinous? Me or you?" She tied the belt around her arm and pulled on it.

I slid across the bed and took the syringe out if her hand. "You can, ma. Let's get you right, then I'll worry about me. Come on."

She handed me her arm, and I rubbed an alcohol pad all

around the site I was looking to inject. After I finished, I took the needle, stuck it into her arm, and pushed down on the dropper, allowing the potion to flow into her system. Her eyes rolled into the back of her head. "Uh, daddy." She tilted her head back and shivered.

I removed the syringe and watched her for a minute. My stomach did somersaults in anticipation of my own euphoric feeling from the China.

Yani sniffled and wiped at her nose, closed her eyes, and smiled. She ran her tongue all over her thick lips. "Damn, baby, I'm pain free again. I hear the music, Heinous. Oh, it's playin' my song, and it's so loud. My body feels so good. Yes, daddy." She leaned back onto her elbows.

I fixed the belt around my arm and pulled it as hard as I could until a thick vein appeared. Once it did, I handled my bidness and pushed down on the dropper as I had with Yani. As soon as the poison rushed into my veins, I felt everything turn hot, and then numb with a vibrating-like contrast. The music started to play loudly inside of my head, and suddenly the anger I was feeling subsided. It gave way to bliss. Bliss from the drug I'd injected into myself. My eyes got low. I felt sleepy and fully awake at the same time. My adrenalin rushed, causing me to stand up.

Yani got out of the bed and walked up to me. She slid her hands over my chest and then pulled up my shirt. "I wanna see your abs, daddy. Ain't nothing like a fine-ass nigga wit' abs. Yo' stomach make me wanna do some nasty shit to you." She pulled my shirt all the way up and off, stood back, and marveled at my stomach muscles. "Now, that's a savage, right there. Bullet wounds, and muscles. Chicago in the building." She laughed, then started to kiss all over my chest.

I reached around her body and gripped that fat-ass booty

that was encased in a pair of tight Dolcé and Gabana's. Her ass was chunky and felt heavy. I pulled upward on the cheeks to get the full effect. "Ma, you losing weight, but this ass is still stupid fat. I wanna lick in between these cheeks. Take these pants off and lay yo' ass on the bed. Hurry up so I can do my thing."

She stood back and wiggled side-to-side in an effort to get her pants down her shapely hips. She got them midway down her thighs and had to get on the bed with her legs in the air to try to get them off the rest of the way.

I rushed her and flipped her over, straddled her body, and scooted down until by nose was right in her ass cheeks. I sniffed, inhaled her perfume, then kissed all over the cheeks, sucking hungrily. The drug had me so horny I felt like fucking her with all of might, but there was another part of me that craved some freaky shit. I wanted some of that fat ass. It had been a while since I'd gotten into that back door, and I was fien'ing for some of it. She was so thick and had always been that way, even with the minor weight lost.

She laid on her hands and spread her legs. The thong sliced her globes down the middle. I pulled the material to the side and exposed her lips, kissed them, and sucked them into my mouth fast, like a vacuum cleaner.

"Un! Heinous! Ooh, daddy! Eat this pussy. That shit feel so good. Eat me, daddy." She spread her thighs wider and tried her best to look over her shoulder at me, but one nip at her clitoris with my teeth sent her shivering as if she was in the freezing snow. She bucked and moved her right thigh to her rib cage, giving me access to attack that monkey.

I sucked, licked, and blew on her clit before sucking it like a juicy berry. Her cream ran out of her and onto the white sheets. I licked it up and swallowed, opened her ass cheeks, and ran my tongue up and down it, kissing the crinkle of her anus and sliding my tongue through her opening. She slid her hand under her belly, and her fingers wound up in her crotch, diddling her clit. I darted my tongue in and out of her back door before licking all over her fingers that were in the way of my path to her clit. "Move 'em, Yani, I got this." I crashed into them with my forehead to get them out if the way.

"Uh! Okay, daddy. But please, make me cum. This dope got my shit going haywire!" She came up on her knees and spread her thighs as wide as they could go before laying her face back on the bed and gripping the sheets. "Daddy. Daddy. Daddy. Uh. Daddy."

I had her clit between my lips with my tongue twirling all around it. There was so much juice coming out of it that it seemed as if she was peeing all over my lips. Her natural scent was heavy. Attacking my nostrils, driving me crazy. My own piece was throbbing so much I had to take him out, and while I ate her pussy and back door, I humped into the sheets. "Cum for yo' daddy, Yani. Make this fat-ass pussy come all over my lips. Make daddy proud." I spread her labia wide and flicked her clit over and over, sucking in between multiple flicks. My face was so greasy it ran down my neck and to my chest.

She balled her fist and started to beat on the bed. "Uh! Uh! Uh! Shit. I'm cumming, daddy. Yo' baby cumming. Aw, fuck!" She popped her ass back into my face and rotated it in a circular motion, shaking like a leaf in autumn and cumming all over my mouth and chin.

I continued to slurp until she stopped shaking, then opened her cheeks and twirled my tongue inside of her anus. I stood up and stroked my pipe up and down, walking across the bed on my knees. "Baby, suck this muthafucka real quick. Get it nice and wet so I can get me some of this ass,"

I ordered, placing my dick right on her lips.

She grabbed it and pulled me closer. "Okay, daddy. You already know I ain't got no problem sucking this big-ass dick. I'm yo' ho, have been since day one. You showed me how to suck dick, daddy."

She sucked me into her mouth and wasted no time sucking me like a porn star. Her jaws hollowed in and out. Her loud slurping and gagging made me shiver and brought me to brink in two minutes' time. When I pulled back, it was dripping with her spit. The head looked like a brown apple.

"There you go, daddy. Now, fuck this big ass." She slapped herself on the ass hard, causing it to jiggle, and laid her face on the bed again in anticipation for me.

I slid the tip into her pussy and dipped inside of her for twenty strokes, then pulled out and began to fit him into her back door.

She arched her back and groaned. "Uh! Daddy!" She slammed backward and took me to the deepest recesses of her ass.

I gripped them hips and stroked her long and fast, going harder and harder while she moaned and begged me to slow down. Her big booty clapped into my lap, tugged, and felt as hot as a sauna. I rubbed all over it while I fucked. Occasionally I'd smack that ass. She'd squeeze, and that motivated me to go deeper.

She played in between her sex lips while I rammed her from the back, pinching and circling her clitoris with her fingers. "Cum in me, daddy. Cum in my ass. Please. Un! Daddy! Yes! Yes! Ooh, that shit hurt so good. Fuck! Cum in me!"

I sped up and smacked that ass as hard as I could. I heard her scream at the top of her lungs and slam back into me.

The bedroom door opened. Carti stepped inside of it with

her hand in her biker shorts and both nipples poking up against her tank top. Her fingers worked overtime in her crotch.

The sight was too much for me. I came, slamming Yani's ass into my lap. Our skins slapped into each other while I jerked and my eyes rolled backward into my head.

Carti eased out of the room just as I pulled out of Yani's back door and fell on my back, my dick still rock hard and throbbing.

Chapter 4

"Mane, before I even got back in town I'd caught wind of that nigga Killa coming up on a major lick. I knew it had to be your scratch, cuz that nigga and his whole crew be about them small bucks. They be robbing niggas for a few ounces at a time, not no major shit. But all if the sudden the nigga buying fully-automatics, like these bitches you see right here, and ten birds of that boy from the same connect I'm fucking wit'. You already know how the streets talk," Crescent said, tooting a line of China hard before turning up a pink Sprite.

He'd gotten back into town two days after he'd initially told Carti he'd be back. That left me in a dilemma because I was close to going at Killa myself because I didn't want that nigga getting comfortable with my cheese. I didn't give a fuck how many fully-automatics he'd bought. In order for him to be able to keep my bread, he was goin to have to kill me. I was a Chicago Windy City nigga to the heart. We believed in money, war, and revenge in the coldest form. I felt like a victim ever since I stepped foot in Dallas. I was tired of the feeling. I was ready to feel like me again.

Crescent was five feet, ten inches tall and dark skinned with a mohawk, curly on top. He was a stocky nigga with a bit of a gut, and for as long as I'd known him he'd been one hell of a dresser and all about his paper. He was Carti's big brother and real overprotective of her because she was his only sibling.

"Nigga, what took you so long to get back to Dallas? That nigga done had damn near a week to spend my bread. Fuck." I picked up a fully-automatic Mach .90 and pulled out the long clip that was filled with armor piercing bullets the color of gold.

"Them right there. I waited two extra days for this crate to come in. I couldn't move until it did. I also had to stop in Arizona for the boy you tooting on. It's the best of the best right now. Seventy percent. That's hard to some by, but one of my homies from the Mala Noche Cartel put me in, and now I'm finna set Dallas up the right way. Don't worry, that nigga Killa ain't gon' go far. He done had the same routine ever since he been in Dallas. He's a bum, a low-life scumbag that ain't got no sense of direction. All he care about is keeping his nose fed and doing petty shit. He brought all them niggas from LA to back him down here. The streets say majority of them niggas are on the run from their plugs 'cause they done ran off wit' packs. Since he been down here, his body count been through the roof, but that's about it. He ain't getting no paper, and if you ain't clocking cheddar in Dallas, then somethin' is seriously wrong wit' you. I say that to say we gon' get your bread back, or whatever's left of it. We gon' have to go to war, though. That nigga's an idiot, but he definitely about that gun smoke." Crescent tooted another line and shook his head.

I stood up and aimed the Mach at the wall, looking through the scope he had attached to it, and zoomed into the roach that was crawling up the wall. The clarity was so good I could see a roach egg hanging out of its ass. "Crescent, I don't give a fuck who this nigga is or what type of toys he playin' wit'. I want my cheese, and I want it tonight. I'm ti'ed of waiting, cuz. Straight-up. So, you need to get right. Make some phone calls so you can tell me where he at. I'll go get him myself. I ain't never needed an army to handle my bidness. I'm a one-man muthafuckin' wrecking crew. Always have been."

Crescent pulled on his nose. "It don't work like that, li'l cuz."

48

I mugged this nigga. "What the fuck you mean?" Now I was getting heated. I was tired of the delays. I was ready to get back what was mine. If I had to start smoking any nigga I assumed was close to him until I got my bread back, then so be it. I could always move away from Dallas. I ain't have no roots there, anyway. Besides, Crescent mentioning the Mala Noche Cartel made me nervous. That was the same Cartel I'd hit while fucking with one of the dirty detectives back in Chicago.

Crescent took a long swallow from his codeine Sprite and burped. "That nigga copping chickens from the same plug I am. That means he's under their protection. He got a li'l crew that's moving units for them. If we fuck with that nigga right now, that's ultimately their operation. We gon' have more than Killa and his crew to answer to, trust me on that. Them Mala Noche niggas is somethin' vicious."

That was the second time he'd brought up Roman Velez's animals from south of the border, the same foes I'd so desperately tried to leave behind in Chicago. "Say, Crescent, how much do you know about the Mala Noche? Is this the same crew of niggas that run under Roman Velez?"

He pulled his nose and swallowed somethin' that was in his throat. "Nall, Roman Velez is only the second in command. His pops is the head muthafucka in charge. You remember when that big-ass caravan of migrants came through from Central America, and President Trump was talking about how he was gon' do everything in his power to keep them from crossing the border? This had to be a few months back in November?"

I separated four lines of China and took one to the head hard. The powdery substance hit the back of my throat and choked me a little bit. I coughed and beat on my chest. The high came right away, more faint than when I banged it into my system, but there nonetheless. It was like drinking a few beers before you started with the hard liquor. "Yeah, I remember that shit. What about it?"

"Well, after they finally started approving their applications to let them in, Roman Velez busted a move and got the soldiers of his cartel approved first. Them, their families, everything. Once they were in the country, they set up stations in New Mexico and dug a tunnel that went right from New Mexico straight back into the heart of their homeland. Through that tunnel they been able to move some major weight and bring the most deadliest of killers over here. But you see, Roman ain't a dumb nigga. Instead of him having his Mexican boys do all of the dirty work, he been plugging into all races and allowing them to kill off their own people by use of his drugs and guns. He been putting plenty niggas on. Muthafuckas wasn't seeing that major cash until he stepped into the picture. But it ain't sweet, though. You see, once you get to fuckin' wit' him, he expect for you to fuck wit' him for life. You try and go into bidness for yourself and it's *pow,* one to the dome." He held his finger and thumb in the shape of a gun to emphasize his point. "But why you ask me that?"

I shook my head. "Just wanted to know, that's all. I heard his name around Chicago a li'l bit before I bounced. No biggie. Life goes on." I sat back on the couch. "Nigga, Killa took all of the bread I had on me. I ain't got a pot to piss in. My bitch offered me a few hunnit from her stash, and I'm more of a man than that, so you already know I ain't going. You expect me to sit back and let this nigga spend all of my cash while I sit around, broke as joke? No, suh. It's either you about to put me up on a lick, or I'm finna use this Mach to sweat that whole scene where his boys be at. Fuck Roman Velez and his cartel. I'm Heinous. I don't fear no man." I

50

stood up and paced back and forth, clenching my jaw in absolute frustration. I didn't like giving niggas passes. My whole life nobody had ever given me one. They always shot to kill and seized every moment to murder me, but real niggas don't die easy. At least that's how I felt.

"Nigga, if you sit yo' ass down and let me finish, I'ma let you know what I was thinking. It could be beneficial to the both of us." He sat back on the couch and lit a Black and Mild cigar.

I reluctantly sat down and laid the Mach on the table right beside the half brick of China Crescent had out on the table. I would have to remind myself to pinch off of it before I went back upstairs with Yani. We had about two grams left of our own stash, and that wouldn't even get us through the night. And I wasn't the type to ask for a handout, even though I was sure he would have given me as much of it as I wanted. I preferred to take it on my own accord. That Chi shit was in me real tough. "What's good, Crescent? I'm all ears.

He scooted to the edge of his sofa, and placed his hands on his knees. "Like I was saying, that fool Roman Velez been putting all type of niggas onto the game and helping them shoot straight to the top, hitting kingpin status almost immediately. Most of these bitch-ass niggas around here don't even deserve them slots, mane. Pussies was bottom feeders." He ran his thumb through his right nostril and pulled it out, looking at it before wiping it on his shirt. "Well, I know what these niggas are holding and where they copping from. I know they stash spots and all of the pussy niggas that's working under them. I say that to say, cuz, you from Chicago. Niggas sleeping on you out here. I want to use you to crush these fuck-boys, and in the process you gon' get rich. You gon' have way more bread than you came here with. Trust me on that. We just gotta be careful because the

Mala Noche is a lethal bunch. Roman find out we the ones crushing his kingpins, it could be a death sentence for us. So, what do you say? You down or what?"

I snatched the pink Sprite off of the table and turned it up. "Nigga, I know you ain't done talking. You have yet to tell me how all of this shit benefits you. I been knowing you most if my life, and one thing I've learned is you're an opportunist. You find ways to move shit around so you can park your whip into it. So tell me, his does this affect you?"

He snickered and tooted a line hard, took the Sprite back, and chugged the rest of it. He sat the empty bottle next to a full one that had already been mixed up. "I want they real estate. Uptown is mine. I wanna supply this bitch and put my niggas in place. The more area I take over, the more money I'll be able to gross. I want uptown all the way through Belmont Park, all the way to West Village. When it's all said and done, I wanna own this portion of my city, and I don't wanna share it with nobody. Not now, not ever. All of the niggas I'ma have you knocking off is the niggas I grew up with in the game. I need these fuck-boys out of the way. The city ain't big enough. You keep all of the money, and I'll buy the work from you. I'll give you five bands for each move, too. You keep the spoils. So, you rolling wit' me or not?"

I broke about four zips off of his half of bird and pushed it to the side. "Yeah, I'ma fuck wit' you. But I need this fo' zones and an advance on the five bands tonight. I wanna get me and my bitch right. You feel me?"

He nodded, went into his pants pockets, and pulled out a knot of hundreds. He counted off fifty of them and handed it to me. "Here you go. We roll out tonight. I wanna take you to one of the clubs so I can show you some shit. You might have to peel a nigga's potato, too, so be ready."

I packed up the China and shrugged my shoulders.

"Cool. I feel out of practice. It's been a while. Give me a few hours. I'll be ready."

***

"Heinous, you mean to tell me you about to jump back on the same shit you used to be on back in the Land? Really?" Yani asked, pacing back and forth in front of me. She acted as if she was stressed out.

I'd given her a brief synopsis of what I planned to do with Crescent to get our chips stacked back up, and ever since then she'd been pacing back and forth, talking crazy. I wanted to choke her li'l pretty ass out. "I really ain't trying to hear that shit you talking, Yani. Unless you got a better idea, this is what it's going to be."

"Damn. Why we just can't get no regular-ass nine-to-five jobs? What's the matter wit' doing shit the right way? Ain't you tired of being on the run? Killing niggas and worrying about when your day is goin' to come? You know the Bible says when you live by the sword, you die by the sword, right?"

I slid the needle into my vein and pushed down on the feeder. As the China eased into my system, it felt like I was having a million orgasms at once. I pulled the needle out of me and closed my eyes. That murder shit was on my mind now. I saw red behind my eyelids, all if the pussies I'd slain in my past. I yearned for a new kill. I wasn't trying to hear shit Yani was talking about. "I been living by the sword since I learned how to kick it up and hold it right. Fuck death and the Reaper. Nall, fuck that. I am the reaper. This is my destiny. I can't run from some shit I was meant to do. I already know it's how I'ma go out, but we can't change what is already written. I'ma keep on turning the page until my chapter end, word to the man upstairs." I reached for her. "Come here and let me suck on these titties before I go."

She batted my hands away. "Stop, Heinous, because I don't think you taking this shit serious. You promised me a better life. You said once we overcame all of that shit back in Chicago, I could be the leader, that you was gon' follow me. That's the only reason I've stayed this far. It's because I thought you were goin' to change. What's good?" She pushed me onto the bed, then turned her back to me.

I fell back and laughed. I was so high it was impossible for me to get angry at her. I had murder on my mind, but I was able to distinguish between the love I had for my woman and the hate I had for the streets. "Baby, how the fuck we gon' get by with the petty-ass change you got left? Had that nigga never hit me for my paper, then following you would have been a bit more easy to do. But he did, so I gotta make it happen. Gotta get us right. Our style of living gotta stay on point."

"Fuck the style of living Heinous! What about our lives? What if somethin' bad happen to you then I'm stuck without yo' psycho-ass? All the way down here in fucking Dallas? Thinking you gon' change. Man, silly fucking me. Ugh." She roles her eyes at me.

I jumped up and snatched her into by embrace, crashed into the wall with her, then sucked on her neck real hard before biting the shit out of her and sucking on it again.

"Stop, Heinous! Get off of me." She pushed at my chest.

"Whose bitch is you? Huh? What nigga walking this earth own this pussy right here? Huh? Who would you die for? And who'd die for you? Tell me!" I bit into her hot flesh and brought my teeth together.

"Uh, you! Daddy, you! I'll die for you, Daddy. Not no other nigga. I love you, Heinous," she hollered, then tears came down her cheeks. "I love you so much, Heinous. I don't want to lose you." She hugged me tighter.

I moved her head backward and held the back of it while our lips sucked all over each other's. I broke the kiss. "I love you, Yani. You my baby. I gotta make shit happen for us. Gotta make sure we don't need for shit. Baby, as soon as I get us right, you can lead the way. I'll follow you. I promise. You hear me?" I sucked all over her lips, then along her neck. I grabbed her ass that was encased inside of some tight, red-laced boy shorts.

She moaned and leaned her head all the way back again, rubbing up and down my back. "You're always doing me like this, Heinous. You always fuckin' up my brain, baby. It's not fair. I swear to God, it ain't fair."

I picked her up and sat her on the dresser, yanking her boy shorts down her thick thighs and off of her ankles. I opened her legs wide before sticking my face between them and sniffing her pussy at point-blank range. Opening her lips, I trapping her clit before driving her through two orgasms that put her ass out like a light.

Hood Rich

Chapter 5

I turned the bottle of Hennessy up and took two big gulps, wiping my mouth with the back of my hand. The China had me feeling real good. I was breezy and in a murderous zone. I felt like all of my senses were on point.

Crescent sat back in the booth that was red leather. We were in Silks, a nightclub located in the uptown district of Dallas. It was a nice-sized club with two levels to it, a big dance floor, and two stages. This night they had some local performer grace the stage, and the club just so happened to be packed to the gills. Me and Crescent sat on the second floor, peering down at the patrons who were partying.

I had so much China in my system that I felt numb. The music was so loud it felt like the speakers were inside my ear canal. Most of the women I'd peeped covered the bare minimum of their bodies. They were damn near naked and thick as hell. From what I saw early, Dallas seemed as if it was the spot to be.

Crescent lit a Black and Mild and inhaled the smoke. "Cuz, this bitch cracking, ain't it? You a long way from Chicago now," he laughed.

I could barely hear him over the music. I took another swallow of Hennessy. "Why the fuck everybody keep saying that to me? Y'all ain't doing shit out here in Dallas that we don't do back home. I mean, the hos may be a li'l thicker, but that's about it. Why you bring me here?"

He looked across the table at me and laughed to himself. I ain't see shit funny. I was broke and irritated. If he didn't put me up on something soon I was ready to loose my top.

"Nigga, calm yo' short temper-ass down. I brought you here for a reason. Before you leave tonight, it's all gon' make sense. Trust that." He picked up a glass of Patron he was sipping on and tossed it back.

The lights in the club went real dim, so dim I could barely see the people on the lower level. Then, all of the sudden, the strobe flashing lights came on and made it seem like everything was moving in slow motion. I'd always hated those lights because it threw my equilibrium off. Two rappers came onto the main stage with bottles of Ace of Spades in their hands. Their music dropped, and they got to going crazy.

"Now I can show you what I want you to see, since everybody paying attention to them. He scooted around the booth, and pointed directly across the dance floor down to a group of niggas fitted in black and white Avirex leather coats. "You see them four studs down there?"

I glared at the group of niggas and watched as they bobbed their heads to the rappers on stage. I wasn't feeling their singing-rap, but apparently the crowd was. The group of niggas acted like they were all into the show. I didn't give a fuck what a nigga was saying on stage. I couldn't ever see myself turning into a groupie. Never. "Yeah, what about 'em?"

"The heavyset nigga in the front. His name Pack. Roman just hit him with four bricks of that good shit yesterday. Street value one-fifty apiece because it's eighty-five percent pure. If he break them bitches down, he gon' more than triple his money like clockwork. On top of fucking wit' Roman and his crew, he fuckin' wit' a few of the white boys out of San Antonio with that glass. Getting bricks of meth for ten racks apiece. He got a shipment in last night. I want that shit. I mean every single crumb. You make that happen, and I'll pop that shit and give you half of the profits. How that sound?"

I gazed down at him again and sized him up real quick.

He looked to be about 280 pounds easy, six feet, five inches or better, and was dressed to the nines with a bald head. The niggas in his circle stood slightly behind him, scanning the crowd, and now and then they'd stop to enjoy the music going on on-stage.

I knew there was a metal detector at the front door of the club, and everybody had to go through it. I didn't know if they were plugged enough to have been able to avoid it, but all it took was Crescent saying a few words to the bouncer, slipping him a few hunnit, and me and him were able to walk around the metal detector. He'd given me a Glock .40, and that bitch was tucked in the waistband of my pants, locked and loaded.

"So, what you saying? You want me to handle this nigga tonight?"

He nodded and took a pull from his cigar. "Gotta get that work up out of him before he break it down, and then get rid of him. On top of that, that nigga rising too fast out here in uptown, so he gotta be crushed. I say smoke his ass like a blunt of loud, and clean out his stash spot. Since we seen these niggas at the club partying, we gon' bounce and meet him back at his trap. That's where he going next."

I looked Pack over again and saw a fine-ass redbone ease in front of him. He wrapped his arms around her and held her while she danced to the music on the stage. "Cuz, how you know he headed to his trap next and not a hotel? That thick-ass bitch guaranteed to rile him up. Look at how she dancing all in his lap and shit." Down below, the red bone bent all the way over, pulled back her skirt just a tad, and moved side-to-side with her ass in his lap. She was crazy strapped. I could see that from where I sat, even with the lights flashing on and off.

Crescent laughed. "You let me worry about where he

headed next. You just handle yo' bidness when he get there. Come on." He got up from his seat and waved for me to follow him.

We left the V.I.P. room and headed down the stairs. Once on the dance floor, we shuffled through the crowd until we wound up in a hallway that led to a back exit. We took that exit and ended up in the parking lot at Crescent's champagne-colored Lexus truck. I got in and sat the Glock on my lap.

"Just so I'm getting this straight, you want me to send this nigga on his way, right?"

Crescent started the whip, and pulled out of the parking lot. "Blow that punk brains all over his trap. The messier, the better. Like I said before, it ain't about to be no kingpins in uptown other than me. He first up, and I want his bitch-ass to be the first down."

I sat back in my seat. "Say no mo'. Let's roll out." I felt my heart skip a beat. I knew it was about to go down, and I couldn't wait. I felt like I needed to smoke something. It had been way too long.

***

Thirty minutes later, under he cusp of darkness, I stepped out of Crescent's truck and closed the door to it as soft as possible. It clicked. I rolled the ski mask down my face and adjusted the black leather gloves on each hand. Crescent had parked in a dark alley littered with all kinda stray cats. Some were incredibly fat while others were so skinny I could see their skeletons underneath their fur. It told me right away that, just like in the streets where you had some niggas eating as good as they could to the point they were obese, the same went for the cats in the alley. The ones that were about that life walked around with big bellies while the pussies seemed to be starving to death. That was the case, or possibly feline AIDS. I didn't know. All I knew was I wasn't about to be one of the ones starving for long. I'd rather meet the reaper head-on than continue starving.

Crescent pointed to a house about thirty yards from where he'd parked. "Cuz, that's his trap, right there. Here go the keys. Go in through the back door. Ain't nobody there right now, trust me. That nigga won't be back until at least an hour, but it could he less. Just set up inside and let me handle everything else. Aw, shit, I almost forgot. Let me see that heater."

I pulled it off of my waist and handed it to him. He backed all the way up against the garage and knelt down, pulled a small metal piece out of his inside jacket pocket, and screwed it onto the barrel of the Glock. "This another reason it took me so long to get back. These bitches right here. Gotta keep them silencers, you feel me?" He screwed it all the way into the barrel, then handed it back to me.

I looked the pistol over and kicked a skinny-ass cat from in front of me. It had walked up on me, meowing, trying to brush up against my ankle. I ain't like cats, or animals period, for that matter. I thought they were nasty.

I put the pistol back on my hip. He handed me a set of keys. "This one'll get you into the back door, and this one'll get you into the actual crib once you go up the stairs. Remember what I said: smoke that nigga and get that work. Everything is in the house. Make him give that shit up. Hit my burner phone when everything is good, and I'ma swoop back and scoop you. Love, fool."

We shook up and he jogged back to his truck, got in, and drove off. His headlights illuminated the dark alley, casting a glow upon what seemed like a hundred filthy cats.

I jogged off, got to the back of the house Crescent had pointed out, hopped the fence, and wound up in the back yard. Once there, I ran across the grass, knelt down by the back door, and looked both ways. It was pitch black and a bit windy.

After making sure everything was good from where I squatted, I stood up and slid the key into the slot, turned it, then pushed the door in. I dashed into the hallway and closed the door. I waited, listening, trying to see if I could hear anything out of the norm. I couldn't.

After chilling for a few minutes, I bounced up and shot up the stairs. I got to the door and slid the key into the lock. The house appeared empty. Someone had left a big, 4D television playing with the sound all the way up. I checked each room of the house as I made my way toward them, finding them empty like the rest of the place.

The living room table was covered with plastic. On top of it was two bricks of China, a box of aluminum foil, two digital scales, and Ziploc bags. I took the black plastic bag out of my underwear and threw both bricks inside of it right away, residue and all. I left a line and tooted it hard, boosting my high.

A few minutes later, I slid into the pantry and waited for Pack to show up with his entourage. The pantry smelled stale as hell, like a dirty mop had graced the floor sometime earlier that day. I waited on one knee impatiently until I heard laughter and a key sliding into the back door I'd come through. I pulled the Glock out of my waistband and got prepared, my heart thumping in my chest like crazy.

The back door swung open, and now I could hear the voices more clearly. "That bitch almost caught me slipping, mane. My whole knot fell out of my pants, and I didn't even know it. When I came out of the bathroom, she was just picking my shit up and thumbing through it. Had I not seen my money clip, I would have been none the wiser." Came a voice I couldn't place."

"Well, you lucky you caught that ho, 'cause if she would have caught you slipping and took that knot, you would have been short on what you owe me. And you should already know what them consequences be," said another voice.

"Yeah, but it's good. I got all twenty racks back. Huh, let me give you your fifteen so I ain't gotta keep looking over my shoulder."

"Thata be in your best interest."

So far I'd clocked two voices. Two voices meant two bodies. I didn't know which voice was Pack, but I was guessing it was the one making the subtle threats, though I couldn't see either man.

"Baby, we should've ate something while we were out. Ain't no food in this damn house, and I ain't trying to fuck wit' that Chinese food from yesterday. That shit had me on the toilet all morning," came a female voice.

"Bitch, you better make a peanut butter and jelly sandwich or something," joked one of the men.

"I don't want no nasty-ass peanut butter and jelly. You got me fucked up."

"Then starve, bitch," came the same male voice that had been sending idle threats. "Fam, let me holler at you in here real quick. We gotta talk some serious business.

"A'ight, let's go."

"But I'm hungry."

They ignored her.

Shit, now that was three people: two niggas and a bitch. This was getting crazy. I waited for a few more minutes to see if I could hear another voice.

Before I could finish my stakeout, the door to the pantry

opened, and the female paused before reaching for the string to activate the light. Before she could, I grabbed her by the throat. She yelped. I pulled her inside and closed the door, placing my lips to her ear. "Look, bitch, I ain't here for you. I come to handle my bidness wit' Pack, but if you make any noise or bring any attention back here to us, I'ma be forced to get at you, too. You understand me? Nod your head if you do."

She nodded.

"A'ight, now I'ma take my hand away from your mouth. But you see this?" I showed her the silenced Glock.

Her eyes got big. She nodded again.

"A'ight, that silencer mean I can knock this head off of your shoulders and they won't hear shit. So, it's in your best interest to cooperate. You dig me?"

She nodded again.

I slowly removed my hand from her mouth. "How many people in this crib, shorty? And keep your voice low."

She started to shake. "Me and two dudes. One of them is Pack. Look, I don't know what he's done to you or why you're here, but I don't have anything to do with it. Please. If you'll let me go, I'll leave right now and won't tell him shit."

"Shush, bitch, you talking too loud." I covered her mouth again. I could feel her hot breath on the palm of my hand.

"KK? KK? Bitch, where you at? We finna order you a pizza. What you want on here?" The knob on the pantry turned and it began to open.

I grabbed KK around the neck and held the banger to her temple just as the door opened. The first thing I saw was a tall, skinny nigga with his shirt off and two gold chains around his neck. He had two pistols on his hip. When he saw how I had KK snatched up, he jumped back and pulled up both pistols. "Aw, shit!"

Before he could get them off of his waist, I let him have it with four quick shots. *Boof. Boof. Boof. Boof.* The Glock jumped in my hand. Fire spit from the barrel as the shells hopped out of it and landed on the floor. The skinny nigga took all face shots, fell backward, and wound up on his side with blood oozing out of the holes in thick globs.

KK screamed into my hand and became hysterical. She jumped up and down, tears running from her eyes, shaking her head side-to-side. I carried her into the living room. When we got there, Pack had a rope around his arm and was just emptying a syringe into his veins. He pulled out the needle and set it on the table. His eyes were closed. He leaned back in his chair, exhaling.

I brought her all the way into the room. "Say, bitch-ass nigga."

His eyes shot open, bucked in disbelief. He reached onto his waist for his pistol.

"Nigga, I wouldn't do that if I was you. Thata get yo' head knocked off like ya man's in the kitchen. I'ma need all of them bricks, both the glass and that China white. Take me to the safes or lose ya life, pa'tna. This your last warning. Hands in the air!"

He held his hands up. "Look, man, you fucking wit' the wrong house. I'm under Roman Velez's protection. This is Mala Noche work."

I aimed and fired, knocking a huge chunk out of his shoulder. He hollered and flew into the wall, leaving bloodstains all over it.

"Bitch-ass nigga, the next one going between your eyes. Now, I need the money and all of the work."

KK was going crazy. Her body shook. She was whimpering so loud I had to sling her ass to the floor.

She crawled backward on her hands away from Pack. "I know where everything at. Please, don't kill me, I'll tell you whatever you need to know. I don't owe him no loyalty."

Blood gushed through Pack's fingers. "Shut up, you dumb bitch. Don't tell that nigga shit. You gon' get me killed by Mala Noche."

I stepped over and grabbed a handful of KK's hair and yanked her head back. "You know where his safes are? Huh?"

She nodded. "Yeah, I know where they are. I know where he installed them and everything. Just please, don't hurt me. I won't say nothin'. This ain't my bidness."

Pack rolled to his side and picked up his gun. He cocked the hammer and aimed it directly at KK. "Punk-ass bitch. I knew I couldn't trust you. I should've –"

Boof. Boof. Boof. Boof. The silenced bullets from the Glock slammed into his forehead and splattered it against his living room wall. KK screamed at the top of her lungs and covered her head.

Pack's legs kicked wildly. He reached for the gun, taking deep breaths. Blood spilled out of his mouth. I couldn't believe the killer in him. There he was with four to the face, and he was still trying to reach for his gun. I admired that before standing over him and pumping him with four more.

I grabbed KK's hair and dragged her across the floor. "Bitch, where are the safes? Hurry up."

"He ain't got no safes. Everything is in the deep freezer. The money and all of his work. I swear to God, it's more than twenty thousand in there. Just take it and go, please."

I tossed her on the floor in front if the deep freezer. She hopped up and began tossing everything out of it. Once a majority of the contents were on the floor, she reached back into it and pulled out a black book bag. She threw it at my feet. "Check it. It's loaded."

I aimed the gun at her. "Nall, bitch, you check it. And hurry up."

She unzipped the bag, opening it far enough to show me the contents. I saw stacks and stacks of money and silver packages. That was all I needed to see.

"Let me ask you something, KK. You got any kids? What's your connection to this nigga?"

She nodded and zipped the bag up. "A little girl. She's two. She's Pack's daughter, but he don't do nothing for her. Please, don't kill me. I'm all she's got." Tears ran down her yellow face. She clasped her fingers together in prayer fashion.

I stood there for a short while, looking down on her. Though the rules of the game told me I wasn't supposed to leave her alive, I made an exception. I would have hated for a nigga to come looking for me, and in the process wound up hurting Yani on the strength. I prayed Jehovah looked down on me and saw I'd given KK a pass, and when He sent the reaper to collect my soul, he would keep this one ordeal in mind.

I took all of the work and left KK wit' five bands. I told her to spend it on her daughter, which she assured me she would, before I tied her hands and bounced out of the back door. The last words out of her mouth were 'thank you.'

Hood Rich

Chapter 6

"Cuz, you been down here for a month, and me and you ain't been out to kick it one time by ourselves. Tonight is the night. Yo' li'l bitch gon' be straight. She been doing her thing at the club, bringing these country boys out here to their knees. I know it's irritating, but you gotta let her do her," Carti said, looking over at me with her purple lips that matched the Roberto Cavili body-hugging dress she was rocking over three-inch Manolos. Her toenails matched her fit as well. Her swag was all the way up top.

"I ain't even want her working in yo' club, but she insisted. She say she want her own money, that she ain't never been the type to depend on no nigga. I had to honor that because it was real. Far as you and I go, what do you have in mind?"

I looked over to her from the passenger seat of her pink-and-black Benz truck. The interior was all white and soft as a new sofa. She had televisions in the back of each headrest, one in the dash, and hanging from the ceiling. The rims were pink and black as well. Seeing her shit made me want to step my own game all the way up.

"I don't know, I just thought we'd roll around and chop it up. I means, unless you got somewhere else to be."

"Nall, I'm easy for a minute. At least until that nigga Crescent get back from Phoenix later on tonight. Whatever you 'bout, I'm 'bout, too."

It was about five in the afternoon on a real cloudy and windy day. Leaves were preparing to fall off of the trees. They had already turned a shade or greenish orange. This day marked the official one-month anniversary of me and Yani coming to Dallas. I had twenty thousand dollars to my name, and I was sitting on a brick of China I was hoping to sell to Crescent when he got back from Phoenix later in the night.

Carti looked over at me and smiled. "You know, I always found yo' ass to be hella cute. I mean, even back when our parents was trying to force the whole cousin thing on us, I knew off the bat it was gon' be hell for me to see you in that light with lusting over you. Then, every time you and I were alone, you always found a way to get yo' hand between my legs, feeling all on my young goodies. Didn't make no sense. I think you just liked making me wet, that's all that was," she giggled.

I looked out of the window and saw her pass a few school buses packed with kids. I was high as a kite, and it was causing me to see some of the things her and I had done as kids in the back of my mind real clear. So clear my dick was getting harder and harder. "Carti, you didn't know it, but you had this thing where you had a habit of sitting wit' yo' li'l legs open, and your pussy was way too fat to be between your legs at that age. So, I just had to touch all over it, taste it, and all that good stuff. Yours was the first piece of pussy I ate and the first pair of titties I sucked. And we was supposed to be cousins? Yeah, right." I had to laugh at that shit.

She slapped me on the shoulder and kept driving. "Dang, you ain't gotta be so blatant with everything." I noticed she had turned a shade of red.

"But it was all good, though. I always thought you was fine as hell, too, growing up, but I never in a million years figured you would grow to be as bad as you are. I mean, you done grew into your head almost and everything."

She busted up laughing and hit me again. "Shut up." She made a left into West Village and sped past the lights. "Are you hungry?"

"Are you paying?" I threw back at her

She rolled her eyes. "I know you love gyros, so I was thinking we shoot to this new Gyro Shack over here in West Village. They sandwiches be off the hook. Killing the ones back in the Windy, you gon' see."

"Yeah, right. I mean, I'm down to go and eat at this place and all of that, especially since you paying. But they definitely ain't got shit on the gyros back home. Them Greek people live and die by their food and would burn Dallas down if they ever heard you talking like that. You should be ashamed of yourself," I added and took a sip from my grape pop.

She smacked her lips. "Boy, you're dramatic as hell. It ain't that serious. We just gon' go and see what they be about. If you like 'em, you like 'em. If you don't, you don't." She rolled her eyes. "I wish a muthafucka would try and burn my shit down because of my opinion. Lord, my cousin is nuts."

I reached over and slid my hand up her dress. "You still on that cousin shit, huh?" The crotch band of her panties was pulled slightly to the right of her labia. The meat felt hot and soft. I grazed it with a finger before pulling the material all the way to one side and trailing my finger up and down her groove.

She clamped her thighs together. "Stop, Heinous. Damn. You always doing something." She removed my hand.

I stuck the wet fingers into my mouth and sucked her juices off of them. "Yeah, I know why you really brought a nigga out."

"Shut up, 'cause I wasn't even thinking about that." She blushed, and her eyes betrayed her lie. She pulled into the parking space in front of the Gyro Shack. "Come on, let me bust yo' head real quick."

Fifteen minutes later she sat across from me with a big smile on her face. "That boy lit, ain't it?"

I had a mouthful of gyro meat and pita bread, chewing wit' my eyes closed. The cook had put extra cucumber sauce and some spicy cheese on mine, and man, it was so fi'e I was lusting off of it. With every chew, the juices would attack my flavor buds and give them an orgasm. I felt like I was in gyro heaven. By far it was the best gyro I'd ever had in my entire life.

I smacked a li'l while longer before I gave her a response. "It's straight. It ain't fuckin' with the Greek heads back in Chicago, though, no suh."

She pursed her lips. "Nigga, yeah right. That shit so good yo' sweating. Stop playin' and give the D they props."

I took another bite and closed my eyes again. I was trying to become one with my sandwich. I stuffed a few French fries in my mouth and everything. "So where we about to go after here?"

She shrugged her shoulders. I was thinking we go chill at Turtle Creek. Just overlook the water and sip on a bottle of Patron. I just wanna be in your company. It's been a while. You cool wit' that?"

"Yeah, that sound like a plan."

We finished up our banging-ass meal and got ready to head out, but before we left I bought two more sandwiches: one for me and one for Yani when she got home from the club. I didn't know if she was hip to the Gyro Shack, but after she bit into the sandwich I was bringing her, she would be.

We hit up the liquor store and wound up parked at Turtle Creek overlooking the water. Carti had a smooth song by Jhené Aiko playing, and it had me in a zone. It didn't take long before the liquor got to coursing through me, and I was feeling lifted. The sun began to set, and it looked so pretty casting its ray of orange over the blue water. Carti's perfume was heavy in the air.

"I use to love sitting on your lap, Heinous. The way you use to hold me all tight and shit. Man, that used to drive me nuts. You was somethin' else." She said this overlooking the sun setting behind the water. There was a slight smile that spread across her face. Her eyes seemed to be dazed and in a faraway place before she closed them and nodded her head up and down to the track that played out of her speakers.

I looked her up and down, and those thick thighs caught my eye again. Carti had always been strapped, but for some reason she was looking real good to me. I think it was the forbidden aspect of it all or something. Either way, her perfume, our conversation, and the location of where we were chilling was getting the better of me. I took my seatbelt from across my chest and glanced over at her again. "C'mere once, Carti." I opened my arms for her.

Once I said this, she opened her eyes and looked over at me with one of the sexiest looks I had ever seen. She sucked on her bottom lip, then popped it out if her mouth. "What?"

I patted my lap. "C'mere."

She unbuckled her seatbelt and came across the console. I let my seat back just a tad before she straddled me. Her dress rose on her soft thighs. Up this close, her perfume got stronger, along with the scent of the conditioner she used for her hair. She felt warm, and just past her right shoulder the sun continued to set.

She gazed into my eyes and was silent for a moment. "Now what?"

I slid my hands up both sides of her thighs, taking her dress along with it. They came under and cupped her ass, massaging the warm flesh. "Damn, you done got so thick.

What they feeding you down here, shorty?"

She snuck her face into the crux of my neck and sniffed before placing her lips onto my vein. "You wanna fuck me now, don't you, Heinous? You want some of this new pussy." She moved from left to right, then made sure her bottom was all in my lap.

"Hell yeah. I'm grown now. I know how to hit this pussy like a man. All that shit we did as kids is out the window. I got that stick for you, ma, trust me." I sucked on her neck.

She arched her back and moaned. "I'm grown, too. It ain't gon' hurt like it used to when I was little. And I'ma let you go all the way in, not just wit' yo' head. Damn, Heinous." She leaned back and pulled the straps of her dress down her shoulders. Her breasts popped out one at a time, first the left breast, then the right. Her nipples covered a majority of the mounds. That was one of the sexiest qualities about her body I'd remembered as a kid: how her areola had always dominated the breast, and when I got her aroused, the nipples would stand out a cool inch. That was hot to me as a twelve-year-old, but looking at them now, attached to her and factoring in how bad she'd gotten, to me they were ten times better.

I squeezed them and pushed them together before sucking her left nipple into my mouth and suckling as if there was milk inside of it. They felt heavy, and oh, so good.

"Uh, Heinous. You sucking my titty again. Uh, just like when we were little." She pressed her ass into my lap and rocked back and forth, pulling her dress all the way up. "Grip this fat ass, too. Please. I want you to grip it. I'm a big girl now."

I gripped that ass and squeezed. My fingers seemed to melt into her skin. "Damn, you thick now. I gotta have some of this pussy. I know it's fi'e. It felt good when we were kids, but you ain't let me go all the way in. Now I wanna tame this ass." I slid my hand all the way under and slid into her valley, playing over the slippery lips that were puffy.

I remembered the first time I'd seen her kitty when we were kids. It had been a hot summer day, and we'd been having a water balloon fight in the back yard of my parents' place. After we'd played around throwing balloons for two hours straight, Carti had dipped off to the guest room to change out of her wet clothes. I'd followed close behind, already knowing where she was headed. I waited a few minutes after she went into the room before I opened the door. There she was, sitting on the edge of the bed with her little thighs wide open, her coochie on full display for my twelve-year-old eyes. She sat looking at me as if she was a deer caught in headlights.

I must've stayed there for thirty seconds before I heard her mother calling my name. That made me close the door and run away with a tent in my wet swim trunks. After seeing her in that state of undress, I made it my business to get her alone so we could play some sort of game that called for me to be the doctor or some type of parent. It wasn't long before I was licking up and down her cleft on the regular and she was begging her parents to bring her over to our house so she could see me, her cousin.

She reached in between us and stood up with her head against the ceiling of the truck. She opened my pants and pulled out my pipe after I took my pistol and set it in the center console. "You remember the first time I did this? Huh? Remember how scared I was?" She licked her lips and squatted down, sniffed all around the head of my dick, and stroked it. "Damn, you strapped now." She pumped her fist and pulled it all the way down, admiring my dick. "Damn, boy." Her tongue traced the head. Her hot breath added to the euphoric feeling of the act.

I watched her pretty ass lick all over me, her electric green eyes peering into my own. I moaned and spread my legs just a bit. "Yeah, I remember. I dared you to put it in your mouth, and you was scared that just putting it in your mouth would get you pregnant, so I had to eat your kitty first. That's when your li'l hair just started growing down there."

She moaned and pumped her fist, opened her mouth wide, and sucked me into it. She covered eighty percent of my dick, then dragged her mouth back up and off of it before licking all over it again. "You used to make me do all type of shit I didn't want to do when I was little. You low-key turned me into a freak. Watch this." She twirled her tongue around my dick, then sucked my whole pipe into her mouth, gagged, and pulled it back out before licking all over it again. She deep-throated me for five minutes straight at full speed. Her big titties bounced up and down on her frame, the nipples heavily erect.

I started to groan, humping into her mouth from the seat. I took ahold of her hair and wrapped my fingers into it, guiding her mouth up and down. It felt so good I was shaking. Her teeth strategically scraped the head, sending tingles through me. My toes curled. Her sucking got sloppier, her lips more tight. She added the pumping of her fist, and that sent me to shaking.

"I'm 'bout to cum, Carti. I'm 'bout to cum. Fuck!" I sat up and slammed her face into my lap. I took ahold of the sides of her head and fucked her mouth while I came in thick globs.

"Mm." She continued to suck and pump me, sucking so hard I could literally feel my seed being pulled out of me. She sat back on her haunches, wiped her mouth. "Yeah, I ain't twelve no mo', huh?"

My dick was coated with her spit. It throbbed up and down and smacked against my belly. "Fuck you doing? Get yo' ass up here and ride me, cuz, straight-up. I know that pussy gotta be just as good."

I grabbed her by the hair and pulled her up until she was kissing all over my lips. At first I wanted to push her face away, but it happened so fast I wound up rolling wit' it. I wanted some of that pussy. Carti was way too strapped and way too fine for me not to hit that shit.

"Uh, damn, Heinous, why you wanna fuck me so bad? How you know all of this gon' fit?" she teased and took ahold of it again, pumping it fast. She straddled my lap, reached under herself, and moved the head up and down in between her sex lips. Her pussy was dripping wet. Oozing.

"Stop playin' wit' me. If it don't fit, we gon' force it." I popped my hips, trying to land inside of her.

She licked along my neck. "Heinous, I'm a boss bitch. I ain't finna let you fuck me in my truck like I'm some lowlife thot. When you get in this pussy, you gon' enjoy it, and we gon' be at a top-notch place, or at least a bed, not no fucking truck."

She allowed my dick to slide past her inner lips, before pulling it back out and climbing off of my lap. She leaned into it and sucked her juices from me, then fixed her titties back into her dress. "Don't worry, I got you." She got behind the steering wheel, fixing her dress. "You okay?"

I sat there with my piece throbbing like crazy. The aroma of her pussy was all in the truck. It smelled good and added fuel to my burning desire for her. "Yo, I swear to God, I feel like taking that shit right now. You got me all kinds of riled up. When you gon' let me fuck?" I knelt down beside her and slid my hand between her legs. Her pudgy pussy was extra slippery.

She removed my hand. "Soon, if you can pry yourself away from that clingy bitch of yours long enough." She rolled her eyes.

I was so heated that I didn't respond. I was seconds away from taking her shit. I replaced my dick and turned the music all the way up, vexed. I took one last glance at her creamy thighs and shook my head. I was gon' get some of that pussy sooner or later.

Chapter 7

Yani woke me up three weeks later by straddling my body and pushing on my chest. "Daddy. Daddy. Wake up. I got something for you."

I slowly opened my eyelids, and a blurry version of her came into view. My head was pounding. I'd just gotten to sleep about four hours prior, and the night before I'd went real hard fuckin' wit' that China. Crescent was still out of town, and every time he told me he was on his way back, something else would come up that prevented his return. I'd been so irritated by his last excuse that all I could do was turn up wit' a bottle of Hennessey and four grams of boy, so this morning I was hung over and nauseous. "Baby, please get off of me. I feel sick as hell right now. Like I gotta puke or something."

She sat back and looked down at me. "Damn, I ain't seen yo' ass in two nights, and that's the only response you got for me? Really?"

She wasn't lying. Yani had been going hard in the club. In the short amount of time she'd been doing her thing in the club, she'd already developed a crazy fan base. She had niggas and bitches driving all the way from Houston and San Antonio to come see her do her thing. She worked the main stage three nights out of the week, and from what she was telling me, the other females at the club hated on her a lot because not only was she stealing their shine, by their money, as well. She gave no fuck. She ain't like them country girls, no way. She was a Chi Town lioness.

"Baby, it ain't that. I just went a li'l hard last night. I'll be a'ight in a minute, but get off of me for now. Please."

She rolled her eyes and climbed off of me. She stood on the side of the bed, shaking her head before walking over to the closet and grabbing her Louis Vuitton bag and taking a big bundle of cash out of it. She threw it on the bed between my legs. "Here, this for you."

I sat all the way up and took ahold of the money. It was mostly fifties and twenties. There were a few hundreds in there, as well as a bunch of tens and ones. "How much is this?"

"That's ten gees. I made that shit last night, and I wasn't even at my best. I gotta tell you, at first I was against all of this 'dancing for niggas' shit, but now I think I'm becoming addicted to the money. I just wanted to hit you off right because whatever I make tonight, I'ma keep for myself. I gotta get my savings back in order. I still got my dreams of becoming a major business and real estate mogul one day soon. I know it take money to make money, so I gotta get right. Is that enough, or do you need a li'l more?" She pulled out another knot. This one was all hundreds.

I sat there looking at her, dumbfounded. I had a few bands to my name before she hit me with the ten, and I'd never felt so down and out. Waiting around for Crescent was starting to attack my ego. I had to get my paper in order. I hated feeling like a dependent. "Nall, this good. I should be able to do my thing with this. I appreciate it, baby."

She turned her back to me, dropped her skirt, and started to look through her closet for something to wear. It was filled with nothing but designer. She'd come a long way, and I'd barely been paying attention. Her ass jiggled in the tight, black lace boy shorts.

"Don't mention it. You already know whatever I got, you got. We in this shit together. Besides, I still feel real shitty about what happened to all of that money you'd came up with before we left Chicago. I already know you had to put some serious work in for it. I know how you get down,

Daddy."

I got out of the bed and felt woozy as hell. My throat was dry, and so was my mouth. My head was spinning like a fan blade. "We ain't gon' cry over that spilled milk no more. I been sitting around, waiting for Crescent, and that's been hampering my ability to come up on my own stash."

Yani interrupted me. "Daddy, I ain't never known you to sit around and wait for somebody to make it happen for you. You've always been a go-getter. Your own man. A leader. I think coming down to Dallas done made you lazy. It's either that or all of that China you're fuckin' wit'. Either way, it's real unattractive because it ain't you."

She continued to look through the closet, not knowing her words had stung the hell out if me. I mugged the back of her head and slowly walked up on her with the money still in my hand. I cocked back and threw the ten racks at her as hard I could. "Bitch, who the fuck you think you talking to?"

She turned around and dropped the outfit she was holding by the hanger. It fell to the carpet. She stepped over it and into my face. "Nigga, don't be throwing shit at me, and watch yo' fucking mouth. I ain't yo' bitch. I don't know who the fuck you think you talking to." Her face balled into an angry snarl.

I mugged her li'l ass. "Watch out. You ain't tough. You think 'cause you whooped a few fat hoez that you can fuck in my bidness now?"

She smacked my hand away. "Look, nigga, I ain't trying to be doing all this shit wit' you today. I thought that li'l cash'd pick you up a li'l bit. All you been doing is sitting on yo' ass while I go out there and make this cash. I feel like I'm the only muthafucka tryna make shit happen, but it's getting old. I think them drugs turning you into the average fien', and I don't give a fuck how you feel about me saying that." She bumped me out of the way. "You better pick that money up, too, and do somethin wit' it." This made her snicker.

I stood there feeling like a scrub-ass nigga. A bum. My bitch was actually jacking on me like I was a peon or something. I got so mad I got to picking up the bills one-by-one and ripping them bitches up. "You think I need this cash? Huh, bitch? You think I done fell off that much that I can't make shit happen for myself? Huh?" More ripping. Every time it resembled confetti, I would throw that shit into her face. Then I'd pick up another batch and repeat the process until I was done.

She stood looking me over. "You're a petty-ass nigga, mad 'cause I'm bread-winning for us right now. Yo' fuck-boy ego won't even let me do my thing. How small of you. Nigga, watch out. I got places to be." She bumped me again, this time so hard I spun a tad. "Hype-ass nigga. Done tore up ten gees he ain't even have. Just stupid." She walked out into the hallway and then into the bathroom across the hall and slammed the door.

I got to pacing back and forth in the room, feeling like smoke was coming from the top of my head. Damn, was I really falling off like that? Did the drugs really have me in the way she was saying they did? Had I become a bum-ass nigga? The typical hype from the hood like we were accustomed to seeing while growing up? I mean, I was jonesing for a hit because I felt I needed it to clear my mind. I knew if I could get that China into my system, then I would be able to think more clearly. I would be able to manage this situation without whooping Yani's ass.

In the moment, all I could think about was getting knee-deep in her ass. I felt like she was getting at me like I was a sucker. Like she no longer remembered how much of a boss

I really was. But then again, I couldn't remember the last time I'd felt like a boss myself. Shit, or even a manager. I felt low. Like scum. I needed a fix.

I reached for my works and opened my stash only to find I had run out. This made me drop into my lowest stage of depression. I got to missing my mother, my sister, and my old man. I felt so alone as I sat on the edge of the bed.

Yani came back into the room with a pink bath towel wrapped around her perfect body. The swells of her breasts threatened to bust out of the top of the towel. She shot daggers at me and turned her nose up. "What's the matter with you?"

I started to itch real bad, especially the spot in the crook if my right arm where I was accustomed to injecting my dope. It felt like bugs were crawling all over it. I dug my nails inside of the skin and scratched hard. "How much China you got on you?" Now my neck was itching, and then my chest. I scratched each place, one after the next.

She sucked her teeth loudly. "Don't worry about it. I got just enough for me. You betta tape that money together and go get you some. I ain't sharing." She took a pair of red lace panties out of the top dresser drawer and stepped into them, dropping the towel and exposing her sexy body. There were a few stretch marks along the back of her thighs. It looked real good.

Now I was itching as if there were fleas crawling all over me. "Yo, Yani, stop playin' wit' me. Give me some of that shit until I can get out the house to go and get my own. And quit talking to me like you don't know who the fuck I am." I scratched the back of my neck so hard it bled.

She shrugged her shoulders. "I'll be damned if I give yo' ungrateful-ass anything. You just set there and ripped up ten gees. If I got anything to do wit' you getting high right now, nigga, you gon' be sick. Whatever you going through, deal wit' that shit." She slid her arms into her bra and situated her breasts so they fit into the cups perfectly. "Matter fact, let me just do my li'l shit right now." She took her Birken bag off of the closet floor and reached inside of it. She came out with a Ziploc bag full if aluminum foil. She dropped the bags and grabbed her tools from the third drawer of the dresser before sitting on the bed, getting ready to handle her bidness.

I watched her for a long time in silence, disbelieving she would treat me as such. This bitch must've thought she was better than me or something, that just because she'd come up on a few pennies, it constituted she was some kind of boss bitch or some shit. I didn't know what was going through her mind, but I was ready to check that shit in.

I stepped out of the room and jogged down the stairs of Carti's crib. "Yo, Carti! Carti, where you at, ma?" I checked the living room, dining room, kitchen, and knocked on her bedroom door. After getting no response, I jogged back up the steps and pushed in the door to the bedroom.

Yani was just sticking the needle into her vein and pushing down on the feeder. As the China entered into her system, she moaned out loud. Her eyes rolled into the back of her head. "Damn, that shit good." She took the syringe and sat it on the nightstand.

I cracked any knuckles. "Bitch, I hope you good and high because, on my mama, I'm about to teach yo' ass a lesson."

She jumped up and threw up her guards. "Long as you know it ain't sweet, let's get it on." She came around the bed and kept her guards in the air. "Come on. Fuck is you waiting on?"

I snapped. I rushed her and grabbed her by the neck, picking her up in the air wit' it while she fucked my face up with heavy blows. I made her head touch the ceiling, them slammed her down with all of my might right on her back.

She bounced off of the carpet and rolled to her side, coughing. Slowly, she made her way to her feet. "I swear to God, I hate you, Heinous. I hate your fuckin' guts. You dope fien'!" She rushed me, swinging wildly with her fists balled. the fingers had a diamond on each one, including the pinky.

"Dope fien'?" I blocked each one of her blows, then slapped the shit out of her so hard she fell to the carpet. "Bitch, you gon' respect me. You think 'cause these country niggas out here sweating you that you ain't still the same ol' Yaniece? Huh?" I picked her up by her hair and slapped her ass again, heated because she was high and I was sick, jonesing for a fix. I felt so belittled, and I needed to bring her down to my level.

She fell to one knee and held her bleeding mouth, looked at her fingers, and then up to me, nodding. "Okay, nigga. I see what this is. You gon' take your emasculation out on me. A'ight. Well, come on, Heinous. Beat me. Beat me until the truth goes away, nigga. This making you feel like a man? The woman that's been riding beside you is on the floor right now, bleeding by your hands. You put me here, and for what? Because that dope got ahold of you?" She stood up and held her arms out like a cross. "Hit me, hype-ass nigga. G'on 'head. You can't break me. I'm a queen, nigga. So hit me!" she screamed.

I raised my hand, prepared to assault her again. Her words wounded my pride, my ego. They brought my reality to the forefront. I had a problem. I was losing myself, and I had to find me before I lost myself completely.

I pushed her out of the way and grabbed the dope off of the nightstand, filled my syringe, and gave myself the much-needed dose of poison. "Fuck what you talking about, Yani. I'ma get my shit together. Just wait, ma. I ain't finna be fuckin' wit' this dope forever. I just gotta find myself. I'm a li'l lost right now, that's all."

The room got cloudy as the drug coursed through my veins. I felt a sudden wave of calm, peace, relaxation, and euphoria. Suddenly, I regretted putting my hands on her. I closed my eyes and drifted for a few minutes. I didn't open them again until I head the familiar sound of *chic-chic*.

Yani stood in front of me with my Glock aimed at my face. Tears ran down her cheeks and dripped off of her small chin. "You think you can put your hands on me and I ain't gon' do shit about it?" Her finger wavered over the trigger.

I swallowed my spit, so high the gun looked blurry. It was like I knew what was going on, but I felt so good that my brain could barely process it. "Bitch, get that gun out of my face or pull the fuckin' trigger. I ain't scared to die. It is what it is."

She wiped a lone tear from her cheek. "I hate you now, Heinous. You ain't the same man no more. I don't know this version of you. I want to kill it." Her bottom lip quivered. Both of her hands shook while holding the piece.

I sniffed and wiped my nose. "Then go for what you know. You better make sure I'm dead, though. The last nigga that thought he killed me but didn't wound up on the receiving end of my wrath. That's a journey you don't need to embark on, shorty. So empty that bitch. Put the holes right here." I pointed to my forehead real hard, so hard I scratched myself. "Hurry up, bitch. Splatter my shit. It ain't that hard!" I grabbed ahold of the gun and pressed my forehead against the barrel to make it easier for her. I was ready to go. I was tired and didn't know how much more I could take. The drugs, the souls of all the people I'd killed, the struggle that lay ahead, being on the run, feeling like shit. I was tired of it all. Fuck death.

She held the gun and started shaking so bad her knees buckled. She fell to both of them and shook her head. "Oh my God, now I know it's true. You done gave up. You gave up, Heinous, and it ain't fair. What the fuck do we do now? Why did you bring us all the way down here? I thought it was for a fresh start. I'm getting the fuck out of here." She dropped the gun and stood up. She grabbed a suitcase out of the closet and began filling it with clothes. "I can't do this no more. I can't do this anymore." Tears rushed out if her eyes worse than before, coupled with snot that slid out of her nostrils and onto her top lip.

I lowered my head, thinking about everything that had transpired. I glanced over at her and felt remorseful. Saw the blood on the carpet from the wound I'd given her, along with the one in her heart. I'd never put my hands on her before, and this time hadn't warranted it, either. Yani was my baby. I was in the wrong, and I was starting to feel sick to the stomach the more she packed. "Yani. Baby. I'm sorry."

She continued to pack. "Don't 'baby' me, Heinous. That shit ain't gon' work. I'm tired. I can't do this shit no more. You're too far gone. There is no saving you. I gotta get out before I lose myself. Gotta get clean and get my life on track. I still got a whole list of goals I have to accomplish for myself. Things have to be about me now. I'm done living for you." She stuffed the suitcase and stood up, opening her dresser drawers and tossing the contents in the bag as well.

I got sicker and sicker. "Baby, please, don't make me beg you. Don't fuck wit' my pride like that." I got up and walked over to her.

She ignored me and continued to pack. Now she was mumbling under her breath. Blood continued to drip from her lip. It ran onto her chin and down her neck. I felt like shit again.

"I don't know how I'm going to make it in Dallas, but I'll figure it out. That's my problem, though. I been way too dependent on you. I gotta get out there and do things on my own. I am more than capable. I am a queen. You ain't gotta tell me that I am. I already know that I am. I am strong. I am more than what the world says I am. My dreams are meant to be conquered and brought into my reality. I am a woman of substance."

I didn't know what the fuck she was saying, but she was scaring me. I didn't want to lose her. Not Yani. Not my first and only love, the only female I had cared about outside of my family for as long as I could remember. I needed her. She was all I had left. I couldn't fathom being without her. We had been through it all together, and because I had been with her, everything had been manageable.

She finished packing and dropped her bags by the door. "I love you, Heinous, but I can't take this shit no more. I hope you have a good life." She grabbed her bags and left out of the door.

I wanted to grab her arm, wanted to beg her to stay, wanted to tell her how much I loved and needed her. But instead I just stood there looking stupid, too stuck in my own ways to fight for her, too stubborn to get back the only person who had ever unconditionally loved me outside of my family.

The sound of her feet going down the stairs sent one dagger through my heart after the next. I fell to my knees, crawled across the carpet, and loaded my syringe with the China she'd left behind. The same China I'd beat her for.

I prepared my vein and injected myself.

Chapter 8

I ran my tongue across my teeth and lowered myself into the passenger seat of Crescent's Benz truck. The seats were all black leather, soft, and the truck still had that new car smell because he'd just copped it a week earlier.

Yani had been missing in action for four weeks. In that time span I'd been hitting up her phone at least ten times a day with no response from her. She had me blocked on all of the social media platforms and had told Carti more than once to tell me she wasn't fuckin' wit' me no more. Then Yani'd give her a bundle of cash, telling her to make sure I got it. That had taken place two weeks ago, and since then I hadn't heard from her, not even through a third party. She hadn't shown up for work at Carti's club since then, either.

I was worried sick about her, and the only way I'd been cooling was to bang seven grams of China a day. My habit had gotten so bad I had to switch arms because the vein in my injection site was no longer present. I felt like I was on the precipice of self-destruction. I just ain't give a fuck no more. I summoned the reaper.

We were parked at Turtle Creek. It was eleven at night, and Crescent was supposed to be meeting up with a buyer who wanted to cop four birds from him. The buyer was supposed to have 120 bands 'cause Crescent wanted thirty apiece for each brick. The only thing about it was Crescent didn't want the nigga holding like that in Uptown, so he wanted me to take his cash and keep it. I ain't see no problem wit' that, especially since I was hurting, anyway.

There was a whole other mess of cars in the parking lot besides ours. It was kind of cold out, but for some reason a bunch of people had chosen to come to the lake that night. We were waiting for a red Porsche truck to pull up. That's what the buyer was supposed to be rolling

"Nigga you good? You ain't said shit since we left the crib an hour ago," Crescent said, twisting the top off of his pink Sprite. He had added double the amount if codeine that he usually did, so his Sprite was more purple-tinged than pink.

I scratched my inner forearm, and sat back in the seat. He was banging that new Moneybagg Yo. That shit was hot to me. "I'm good. I'm just ready to handle this bidness. I could use that li'l scratch. Ain't no telling when you gon' up and shoot out of town again, leaving a nigga in the lurches." I mugged him and looked past his shoulder, out to the series of cars that were parked in the parking lot. Some of the windows to a few cars were steamed up. Some rocked back and forth. Some had smoke coming out of the windows while on other cars and trucks people were sitting in front if them, booed up.

"Nigga, that's the way of the world. You can't make no money sitting in one place. You gotta navigate all over the states. That's the only way you can make the most amount of cheese. Niggas that stay still stay broke."

I shot daggers at this nigga. "Yeah, well, I said what I said. Let's just handle as much bidness as we can before you take another trip. I need to get my weight up."

"Fo' sho. A'ight, now remember, he gon' pull up in about five minutes. I'ma tap my horn, and then he gon' follow us to a spot of my choosing. I'ma lead him down to the old bus station repair warehouse. Once we get there I'ma jump out and fuck wit' him to make sure that paper is right. Once I confirm he got that gwop on him, I'ma make my way back to the whip as if I'm about to grab the work, and that's when you jump out and lay his ass down and out. I'm talking fatality. You can keep the whole one twenty, and I got six zips of some Korean Boy for you. This shit straight from Kim Jong-Un's personal stash," he laughed and pulled his nose. He had a real habit of doing that.

I heard everything he'd said, but I couldn't help but think about Yani. I was missing her like crazy. I wondered if she was okay. Had she gone back to Chicago? Or maybe out east? I silently prayed I'd see her again soon, that she would unblock me so we could work things out. I needed my queen. Shit was too real without her. I didn't know how strong a woman made a man until I'd lost mine.

"Yeah, I'ma need to get my shit, too. I need all six. Now, what happens if this nigga ain't got the one twenty? What if he on the same snake shit you're on? That bet' not affect my pay. I need all of mine, straight-up." I took the Mach .90 from under my seat and set it on my lap. It was a fully automatic. One tap of the trigger and it would spray rapid, three bullets at a time. I twisted the cap off if the codeine and downed the whole Sprite without stopping. Crescent had me hooked on it. Whenever it mixed with the China, it put me in a murderous mood. I was ready to spill a nigga's brains.

Crescent shook his head. "This nigga wouldn't play witness like that. He know I'm about my scratch, and if it come down to it, I'll wet a nigga up like a sprinkler. I ain't always been the nigga calling hits. I used to be the one doing them, too." He shook up the Flonase bottle filled with heroin and water, then snorted it up his nostrils one at a time. "This fuck-nigga gon' have my scratch. He want this product because he trying to take over Oak Grove Avenue and Clyde Lane, but I ain't going. To the dirt he goes, along with the rest of the niggas that's impeding on my turf. I am uptown. Ain't no nigga gon' survive these slums but me."

I looked over at him and scoffed. "Fuck you so obsessed wit' uptown for? This muthafucka ain't all that."

He mugged me and was about to explain himself when a pair of headlights shined into our truck, damn near blinding me. "A'ight, cuz, slide all the way down. It's show time."

I was already ducked low in the seat, but I slid even further to the ground. The hunnit-round clip of the Mach .90 hung out of it like a table leg. I had another one in my pocket, and if I had to, I was going to use both of them.

Crescent hit his horn twice, then backed out of his parking space. I rolled the mask down over my face and closed my eyes. Yani's face entered my mind's eye. Her beautiful smile, the way she looked stepping out of the shower, all natural and perfect to me. I missed the way she felt in my arms, our conversations, arguments, and rough sex. She was my equal, no doubt. I wished I would have cherished her more, wished I'd never started fucking with the heroin.

"Li'l cuz, it look like he got somebody rolling wit' him, too. I should have expected that. This bitch-nigga so scary, but what else is new? Make sure you clap his passenger, too. I'll make sure I hit you for that. In fact, I'ma give you one of them North Korean bricks. That'll gross you seventy-five gees on the street. It's ninety-five percent. I'll vouch for that." He turned onto a highway and sped up.

"Sound good to me." I didn't give a fuck about smoking somebody else as long as the pay was right. I had so many souls haunting me at night already that one extra one couldn't do that much damage. It was what it was. I needed as much money as possible. That was all that mattered to me.

"You asked me earlier why I care about uptown so much? I know you probably don't remember, but my pops was killed out here about three years ago, back in 2015. He was trying to do the same shit I am right now. Trying to sew this bitch up. His blood, sweat, and tears are all over the concrete, and mines is, too. A lot of these bitch niggas' old men facilitated my pops' murder, so I ain't got no love for none of them. Fuck all these niggas. Uptown is mine."

That shit sounded real psychotic to me, but as long as I was getting paid, I didn't give no fuck. I would knock heads off left and right. I couldn't sleep at night, anyway. There were so many spirits harassing me that I'd given up.

I felt the truck slowing down. "What the fuck going on?"

"I'm hitting this exit. The old bus station warehouse is about three blocks from here. Just stay low. We about to get this nigga."

I put my gloves on and curled my upper lip. I needed that bread. I was tired of feeling like a bum. I needed the money just to feel like I was back on bidness. Lord knows it had been a minute.

"Man, cuz, I'm glad you fuckin' wit' me in this shit, too. You so one-hunnit. I got some other shit I'ma put you up on when it fall through, something that should set you straight for a long-ass time. Just keep fuckin' wit' me."

"Save them pipe dreams for them naïve-ass hos you be fucking wit'. I fuck wit' facts! Let's just handle this shit and go from there." I ain't wanna hear that jive the fool was talking. I knew he didn't do shit unless it benefitted him, so I was curious to see what he had up his sleeve. One thing for sure was I never took nothing Crescent said at face value. I always made sure I looked beyond the surface of what came out of his mouth. I knew I wouldn't be riding under his thumb for long. I was a born boss, regardless of the drug usage. I was just waiting on my moment. I wouldn't be down for long.

He pulled into the back of the old bus station repair warehouse right off of McKinney Avenue and threw the truck in park. "Bruh, as soon as I come back and open the driver door, I want you to do your thing. In fact, I'ma bring that nigga back to the truck wit' me so you can hit 'im up. Just make sure you wet his passenger, too. I'll be right back." He opened the door to the truck and hopped out with a mug on his face and a Glock .9 in his waistband.

I could hear the sound of his boots crunching on the rocks and another car door slam in the distance, but I didn't look up because I didn't want to blow my cover. I stayed ducked down, waiting patiently. The palms of my hands were itching, and so was the skin under my mask. I was ready to go, but knew I had to wait for him to come back.

Once again, my mind drifted to thoughts of Yani. I wondered if she was okay. If the China had taken ahold of her or if she'd been able to kick it. I wondered if she was fucking wit' another nigga, letting him hit the pussy and all that good shit? I wondered, if there was another nigga in the picture, if she loved him as much as she did me once upon a time. I missed my woman, and whenever I imagined another nigga doin' the things to her I used to, it made me want to kill something. "Damn, I miss you, Yani. I'ma change, boo. I swear to God, I'ma change," I said out loud, and I wanted to mean that with every fiber of my being. I wanted my baby back. Bullshit wasn't about nothing.

That's when I heard the sound of more than one pair of shoes stepping over the gravel. I slid lower to the floor mat, then climbed to the back of the truck as quickly as I could. As soon as I got back there, the driver's door opened and Crescent stuck his head in, laughing.

"Nigga, I know all one hunnit and twenty thousand better be in that bag, or me and you gon' have a problem," he said, reached into his console and looking back at me. "Do ya thing, li'l cuz. Smoke this nigga."

I ain't waste no time. I opened the back door and jumped

out. The buyer stood about five feet, nine inches tall. He had a neck full of jewelry and looked like he weighed every bit of three hundred pounds. His dreads were down to his waist.

When he saw me hop out of the back door, he drooped the bottle of Sprite he was sipping on. "Aw, shit, mane. Crescent, you set me up. You dirty-ass nigga!"

Bop. Bop. Bop. Bop. Bop. Bop. Bop. Bop. The Mach jumped in my hand and spit shell casings into the air. They fell to the ground and made a loud tinkling sound. The bullets shredded the buyer's face. I watched them go into his meat and knock big chunks out of it before he shook and fell to the ground in a sea of burgundy.

"His passenger, too, cuz. That nigga gotta go, too," Crescent hollered and jumped behind the wheel of his truck. "That bread on the back seat. Get that shit."

Before I could get to the buyer's car, it backed out of the parking lot and crashed into the front bumper of Crescent's truck, rocking it. The sound of crunching metal resonated loudly. Crescent's headlight shattered and went dark. Through Crescent's windshield, I saw him slam both of his hands on the steering wheel in anger. The driver of the buyer's car struggled to back up again.

When the collision had occurred, I'd jumped out of the way and bumped into the big metal dumpster that sat outside of the warehouse. The handle the garbage trucks used to scoop the dumpster had punched me in the back, causing me to double over briefly, but now I'd gotten my footing. I tightened my grip on the big Mach and rushed around the back of the car as quickly as I could. The driver stepped on the gas, and his car untangled from Crescent's truck. His bumper hung like an elephant's trunk, scraping along the pavement with sparks flying up from it. I stopped and busted out the back window. *Bop. Bop.* It shattered. The glass spilled all over the back bumper. I could hear whimpering coming from inside the car. The driver seemed to be as big as the buyer had been. I wondered if they were related.

"Finish him, cuz, and come on. This nigga done fucked up my shit. Man, finish that nigga!" Crescent hollered with his head sticking out of the window of his truck.

I rushed all the way around and yanked on the handle to the car, and to my surprise it opened.

The driver sobbed, "The money back-back thur, mane. Take that shit. It's on the back seat. Ain't nobody gotta die for this shit!" Blood gushed out of his shoulder blade. He inhaled and exhaled loudly, almost as if he was having some sort of asthma attack.

He tried to turn the wheel to direct the car past the big dumpster, but his car clipped it. I stood back, then rushed him again. I stuck the Mach right up to his sweaty neck, pulled the hairpin trigger, and held it. *Bop. Bop. Bop. Bop.* The bullets ate through the flesh and left the windshield spattered with his blood. The windshield and my mask.

He slumped over to the passenger's seat, his eyes wide open and unseeing. I grabbed the bag of money off the back seat and jumped back into Crescent's truck before he stormed away from the scene, cursing about having just copped the truck and already it was ruined. He sounded like a straight bitch. Had he not been my cousin I would've smoked his ass, too. Facts!

Chapter 9

Yani showed back up two weeks after the ordeal at the bus repair warehouse. Crescent and I were sitting on the porch sipping on a bottle of Patron when this black-and-purple 2020 BMW truck pulled up to the curb in front of the house with mirror tints on it. The paint had the Louis Vuitton logo all through it.

When I first saw it, I jumped up and slid my hand under my shirt, cupping the handle of my ten-shot .45. before I backed toward the house. Crescent somehow got behind me and dropped the bottle we'd been sipping on.

"Mane, who the fuck is that?" he asked, opening the door to the house and was halfway inside of it.

"I don't know, but they can get these bullets sent first class." I cocked the .45 and jumped off of the porch with the pistol at my side.

It was around six in the afternoon on a cool day. Even though the sun was out, it felt cold and had been windy the entire day. There were only a few people sitting on their porches, and they were at the other end of the block. I could see them from where I stood on the porch.

Crescent eased into the house, closing the door. I could have sworn I heard it lock. I threw my hands in the air and waited on the truck to bust a move. I was already in a foul mood. I'd been up all night, unable to get a wink of sleep. All of the souls from the many people I'd slain felt as if they were haunting me. Every time I closed my eyes for more than a few minutes, I was being accosted. I'd wake up in cold sweats with my heart beating fast. I was tired of it, so I'd stayed up, getting higher than Mars.

"What's good?" I hollered, walking toward the truck on some death wish shit. I was seconds away from airing it out.

When I got about five feet from the passenger's side, the window rolled down. This made me jump back, ready to fire. I raised my gun and aimed, then Yani called my name.

"Heinous! You bet' not shoot up my truck, boy!"

The sound of her voice melted me. I tucked the fo'-nickel back into the small of my back and bent over to look inside of the truck. "Aw, shit, Yani. Ma, is that you?"

She rolled the window all the way down. "Yeah, it's me. Get yo' ass in. I need ta holler at you about something."

Crescent opened the door to the house and came back onto the porch. "Heinous, who the fuck is that?"

I waved his soft-ass off. I coulda sworn he locked the front door. I wasn't sure, but I still felt some type of way. "Nigga, it's good. I'll be back in a minute."

I slid into Yani's soft leather seats, and as I closed the door, the seatbelt wrapped around me and clicked into place. She drove away from the curb, the truck navigating with a light humming sound. The drive was smooth. The dashboard looked like a spaceship. The scent of her perfume was heavy in the closed space. I loved every whiff of it. She had her hair curled. Her make up was flawless and made her look like a celebrity. Her face looked fuller, but sexy. There was no bags under her eyes like there had been the last time I'd seen her. Her lips looked more juicy and plump. They were shiny. She had my attention. I found myself lusting after her as if I'd never seen her before. Like she was new pussy.

I broke the silence. "Where you been at, Yani? Got me going weeks and weeks all worried about yo' ass and shit. That ain't cool."

She continued to drive in silence, turned on her blinker, and made a left, driving around the block. "I made a pit stop at rehab and kicked that habit that look like it's killing you. I couldn't allow for the devil to control me like that. It took a month, but I kicked that shit cold turkey. I'm clean, and I'm on my bidness now. I'm about to come up in a major way. Mark those words." She had a track by Nicki Minaj and Lil Wayne banging out of her speakers: "Rich Sex."

"Where you get this truck from? What type of nigga you dealing wit' that got you rolling a BMW?"

"How you know it's a nigga? It could be a female. We do run the world, you know." She looked over at me and smiled.

"Stop playin' wit' me and answer the fuckin' question," I snapped.

She rolled her eyes. "Damn, Heinous. I ain't seen you in forever, and you still treat me like shit. I don't get it. Did you at least miss me?"

"Yani, on my mother, rest her soul, if you don't tell me where you been and who gave you this truck, I'ma take this muthafucka right here and blow yo' shit back. Now, keep playin' wit' me." I took the .45 out of my pants and sat it on my lap after re-cocking it. I sniffed and looked over at her.

She continued to drive and exhaled. "Damn, Heinous, I still love yo' stupid ass. I don't know why, but I do." She shook her head. "I been doing my thing in Houston. The clubs are way better over there. The tricks pay more, and I've ran into so many rich people that are obsessed with little ol' me that it's crazy. A fine li'l Mexican princess bought me this truck for my birthday. No strings. She just wants me to dance for her whenever I'm in Houston, and if she can't wait until I travel out that way, she'll fly me out or send for me, no matter where I am. That's it. You wouldn't believe how many other offers I've gotten like that. There have been so many people throwing money and opportunities at my feet that I can't keep up with them all."

"Yani, why do you have me blocked all over social

media? Why you ain't been responding to my texts? Do you know how worried I was about you? Do you?" I was so heated by the things she was saying. Heated because I could tell she no longer needed me. She could survive on her own, and I think a major part of me needed her to actually need me to be her provider. Even though she'd had her own small businesses back in Chicago, that never stopped me from being her center. She looked to me for strength, guidance, and love. I wanted that old thing back. That old feeling. I hated seeing that she was doing so good, especially when I felt and looked like shit. I was stressing, and I knew it.

"Blocking you is what I needed to do for myself. You were my enabler."

"Your what?"

"Enabler. The person who helped me stay on the dangerous path I was on. Every time you did some of that China stuff, I felt like I needed to. Every time you told me to jump, I did. I followed you because you were my man. You was the head, and your guidance led me upon a path of destruction. You were, to put it simple, my enabler."

She pulled the truck into a parking spot in Turtle Creek. The parking lot was secluded. We were the only ones there. In the distance I could see four joggers running along the water. The wind seemed to pick up drastically. It caused her truck to sway.

"Shorty, I don't know what bullshit them people put into your head, but I wasn't enabling shit. Everything you did, you did on your own accord. I hope you wasn't in there trashing me and all of that shit, blaming all of your shortcomings on me. I mean, after all, you are a grown-ass woman."

She turned the key all the way backward so the music played and the heat continued to blow. She took off her seatbelt and looked over at me. "If I would have blamed all of my shortcomings on you, I would have been well within my rights to do so. You put that bullshit in my system by force. You took me out of my comfort zone. You brought me out here. You whooped my ass. You treated me less than human. If you were not the cause of all of my issues, you are definitely responsible for ninety-five percent of them, if not more. So don't tell me what you hoped I didn't do. I did everything I needed to do to get better." She frowned, reached out her hand, and touched my face. "Baby, you look horrible. Can't you see you need to find some help, too?"

I allowed her to stroke my face for a bit before I knocked it away. "You don't give a fuck about me, because if you did, you would have never left. I thought it was supposed to be you and I against the world, but look at how stuck-up you done become with your li'l BMW truck and jewelry all over you like you're some kind of princess or something. Talking all down to me. And before you left, you called me all kinds of hype and dope fien'. Now you wanna sit here and make it seem like everything is cool? Like you really give a fuck about this nigga right here? Man, fuck you, shorty. Straight-up. Fuck you and the horse you galloped in on."

I was so high and my thoughts were so clouded that I couldn't begin to make sense of what I was saying. All I knew was I was jealous. I was missing her. I wanted her back, but the ignorant killer in me wouldn't allow me to bow down to her. I couldn't submit. I was too cold internally for that, even though I wanted to with every fiber if my being. I wanted Yani back bad.

She turned so she could fully face me and slapped her right hand on her thick thigh. This made it jiggle inside of her Prada jeans. "Nall, nigga, fuck you. You see, if anybody don't care about somebody, it's yo' black-ass. Nigga, you don't give a fuck about me. I mean, how could you when you're the one getting me hooked on heroin and shit? Ever since I stepped off of the porch gave you my hand, you ain't been nothing but a pull-me-down. A lowlife thug. Nigga, you ain't got no goals. No ambition. No dreams that aren't outside of the streets. You're stagnant, and you're cancerous to a boss bitch's growth. I'm just being honest. I can't go in no direction but down with your trifling-ass, so fuck you."

I lost it. I grabbed her by her neck with my right hand and squeezed as hard as I could. She gagged and attacked me with her swinging fists. This made me add my second hand. The squeezing got harder and harder. "Bitch, who the fuck you think you talking to? Huh? Who do you think you talking to? You belong to me. You think you better than me now? Huh?"

She continued to fight, gagging and trying to kick at me. "Stop! Ack. Ack. Ack." More swinging with her fists. "I. Can't. Breathe!"

I dragged her ass from the driver's seat and into the very back seat, straddled her, and yanked her arm out of her Prada sweater. "Bitch, you think you don't need this shit no more, huh? 'Cause you kicked? That's what's making you act all boujee?" I took a syringe out if my inside coat pocket. My habit was so bad I kept one there, filled at all times. I couldn't be without the drug. Crescent had put me onto the North Korean heroin, and it was so potent I couldn't go more than an hour without shooting up or my body would start to betray me. I would be in physical pain, all in my stomach, my head, my chest, everywhere that mattered. Places that broke me down like fractions.

I sat on Yani's chest and trapped her right arm, put the wrist under my knee, and flicked the body of the syringe. The liquid inside it swished around.

"Please, Heinous. Don't do this. Please. I don't need that shit back in my system. It almost killed me last time. I'm sorry. I'll go. I'll never bother you again. I promise."

I pulled the cap off the needle with my mouth and blew it out and onto the truck's floor. "Nall, bitch. I'm tired of you flexing on me. Tired of your li'l snide comments. Bring yo' ass back over to the dark side. Back over to daddy, where I run shit." I guided the needle point into her vein and pushed down on the feeder, giving it to her nice and slow as if I was making love to her vein.

"No!" she hollered with her eyes bucked. She made one last attempt to swing at me with her left hand before her eyes rolled into the back of her head. She closed her eyelids and moaned. "I hate you."

I knew from personal experience the North Korean dope was slowly overtaking her body. It would be a new feel to her, way more potent than that China. The North Korean would break her ass down like fractions, make her vulnerable. She would need me in order to have it, and that's what I needed. I needed her to need me again, and if hooking her back into the work was the way to make that happen, then it's what I would have to do.

I slowly got from atop her and knelt beside her. Her chest heaved up and down. There was a little drool in the left corner of her mouth. Her eyelids were closed so tight that all they looked like were wrinkles. I leaned down and licked the drool from her face, swallowed it, and kissed her soft cheek. "How do you feel, baby?" I sucked on her neck and allowed her perfume to drift up my nose. She smelled so fucking good, like the old Yani. The gangsta bitch I had fallen in love wit' back in Chicago as a youngin.

Her voice was hoarse. "I can't believe you did this to me. Why, Heinous? I thought you loved me."

I pulled her blouse up over her arms and off and unhooked her bra in the front. Her pretty caramel titties spilled out. I had missed them so bad. My lips made contact with the nipples, sucked on them one at a time until they were erect, then I was licking circles all around them. "I do love you, Yani. You belong to me. I'm daddy. You can't leave me in this dark cave all alone, baby. You have to be here with me. You just have to."

I picked her up and sat her on the spacious back seat. She scooted backward and groaned. Her eyes remained closed. "I'm too high, Heinous. I can't handle being this high. My heart is beating so fast. I think I need help."

I pulled her pants off of her thick thighs and down to her ankles. Once there, I took my tongue and trailed it along her inner left thigh. I stayed with the path until I got to the crotch band of her pussy-packed panties. I stuck my nose on it and sniffed hard, as if it was a line of that boy or something. Her scent was incredibly strong.

"Heinous. My heart. Baby. My heart is hurting. Can you hear me?" She muttered these words barely above a whisper.

I yanked her panties to the side so hard I ripped them. Since the material was already ripped, I decided to pull it the rest of the way off. I threw it to the truck's floor and opened her thighs. Her pussy sat in the furrow of her gap, bald and juicy. A tingle traveled through me. I began to shake. I stuck my head right into the apex of her center and sucked her lips into my mouth hard.

"Uh! Heinous. Fuck. I can't breathe. I can't." She fell forward onto me and began to shake all crazy. "Argh!" Foam bubbled in her mouth before it spilled over and ran down her chin.

I got up and started to panic. "Aw, shit. Aw, shit. Yani!"

She lay on her side, shaking and convulsing. More foam

bubbled out of her mouth. Her eyes blinked over and over. Her fingers were crooked and locked. Her feet kicked behind her as if she were a dolphin.

"Jehovah, please, no. Please don't let my shorty die. I'm sorry, man. Damn!" I pulled her into my arms, and it was like the seizing got worst.

What the fuck had I done?

Hood Rich

Chapter 10

I sat on the couch in Yani's hospital room with my head bowed. This was the third day I'd been there, and she had yet to wake up out of the drug-induced coma they'd placed her in. It turned out the North Korean work had been too much for her to handle. I'd given here way more than I should have. The dosage had been nearly lethal. I'd gotten her to the hospital just in time. Ten minutes later and she would have been a goner.

I raised my head just in time to see her kick her foot, then she jerked and her eyes popped open. They had her hooked up to all kinds of IVs, and there was a breathing tube down her throat. As soon as I saw her eyes pop open, I ran over to the bed and took her hand. The sounds of the breathing machine sucking and exhaling air for her was loud in the room. So was the constant beeping of the other machines.

"Baby, I'm sorry. I don't know what I was thinking. I swear to God, I'll never do nothing like this again. I love you so much. Can you please forgive me?"

In response, she started to shake. Her eyes blinked faster and faster, then one of the machines started to scream. I jumped back and looked them over. What the fuck happened?

Yani continued to shake, kicking her feet. She sounded like she was choking. Her eyes continued to blink like crazy.

"Somebody, help my woman! Help! Something ain't right!" I yelled as loud as I could.

A bunch of nurses and doctors ran into the room. One of them, a short Indian lady, took ahold of my arm and led me out of the room. "I'm sorry but you'll have to wait in the waiting area with the rest of the visitors."

I moved her out of the way. "Bitch, move! That's my

woman in there."

She ran back and blocked the door, then held up her hands at shoulder level. "Sir, I get that, but she's gone through a lot. You have to let us do what we can to save her. Please. You being this aggressive will only make things worse."

I saw two security guards jogging down the hall, headed in our direction. I also saw the two cameras angled to monitor the hallway and thought better than to make things worse than they'd already gotten.

"A'ight, but as soon as y'all know anything, tell them to contact her emergency contact person. That's an order." I tried to rubberneck over her shoulder to see what I could see. It appeared all of the personnel had surrounded her and were busy at work. That terrified me.

"Sir, you have my word. As soon as we know anything for certain, you will be the first to know. Now, please. Go. I'd hate to see you apprehended over the care you have for this patient."

"Her name is Yaniece. Not 'patient,'" I snapped.

The security guards ran up and stopped in front of us. One of them, some big, black, gorilla-looking-ass nigga, came huffing and puffing in our face. "Is there a problem over here, Nurse Prilonka?"

She waved them off. "No, he's just a bit worried about his girlfriend. Everything is okay. Right, dear?"

I turned my back on all three of them and walked away. What the fuck had I done to my woman?

***

Yani slipped into a coma that night, and after I got word of that, I sat in Carti's guestroom with an ounce of North

Korean in front of me, banging one gram after the next until I was so high I couldn't feel any emotional pain anymore. All I could hear was loud music. My mouth was dry, my throat hurt, and all I could see was the vision of Yani's face playing over in my mind with all of the machines hooked up to her.

I took the .38 Special off the bed, put two in the chamber, and spun the cylinder before snapping it closed. I cocked the hammer, placed the barrel to my right temple, and squeezed the trigger.

Click!

I took a swallow of the Hennessey and spun the chamber again before repeating the same process. It was my fault she had slipped into a coma. My fault for getting her hooked in the first place. My fault for bringing her to Dallas. My fault for being a doped-out lowlife like she'd basically called me. I didn't deserve to be alive any longer. I was ready to meet the reaper. I had a lot to say to his bitch-ass.

I placed the barrel to my temple and pulled the trigger twice. *Click! Click!* Sweat rolled off of my brow and onto my neck. More images of Yani came across my mental, then images of my mother, sister, and father. The pain began to well up inside of me again. I needed more of the North Korean, needed to block the path of pain that was shooting up from my brain.

I grabbed my works and filled the syringe with more of the potent drug, ready to shoot it into my system. The injection site still bled from the usage forty-five minutes ago. I paid it no mind, banging the poison into me again as a lone tear slid down my cheek. I wiped it away with anger. Now wasn't the time to be soft. I had to be strong. Had to be me. Fuck pain. Pain was for pussy-niggas who refused to lay in the beds they had made. I was tired and ready to snuggle up in the blankets of my bed. I couldn't allow myself to simp out like a soft nigga. I had to live with the choices I had made. Crying wasn't gon' get me nowhere, so I stopped it.

There was a knock on my door, then the knob started to turn before I could answer it. It was locked, and thank God it was. The banging commenced. "Heinous. Open the door and let me holler at you real quick. Damn. You been in there all day," Carti yelled. She sounded impatient and irritated.

I ran around the room, trying to clean it up as best I could. I made sure none of the drug shit was out in the open. I didn't think she knew how down in the dumps I was, and if that was the case, I didn't want to promote anything.

It took me two minutes before I opened the door and walked away from it. She stepped inside and held her nose before stepping back out. "Damn, you stank. Un-uh, Heinous. Look, I know you stressing, but you gotta get yo' ass in the tub. You gotta get out of this room. You're killing yourself in here."

I waved her off and sat on the bed. "Man, fuck outside. Yani in a coma. Shit is all fucked up right now. I can't even think straight." I grabbed the bottle of Hennessey off the nightstand, and got to downing it like an alcoholic.

Carti stepped back into the room after dipping in and out if the bathroom while I was talking. She came back spraying a bottle of Febreeze. "Come on, you about to get yo' ass in the tub. I'ma wash you up, and then we're going to the Dallas Cowboy game. They playing the New Orleans Saints, and our tickets are right on the fifty-yard line. It'll help you take your mind off Yani for a minute. Get up, 'cause you going. You ain't got no say-so in this."

As much as I wanted to argue with her, I knew I needed to get my ass in some type of water. I hadn't bathed or showered in, like, four days. I felt gross and horrible. I was usually one if them type of niggas who took two showers a days and stayed fresh at all times, but as of late I just didn't have the motivation to get fresh. I was at my lowest stage of depression. On top of the four days without bathing, it had been almost three days since I'd eaten a solid meal. Whenever I had something to eat it, consisted of a couple of Snickers bars, and then I'd call it a night. My appetite was nonexistent.

Somehow, some way, Carti led me to the tub and had me sit in the bath water she'd filled nearly to the rim. She added some different types of concoctions that had the water smelling good while it bubbled all around me. She took a hand towel and washed me up like I was a little baby or something.

"Heinous, you gotta be stronger than this. I can't believe you letting that shit wit' that girl break you down like a li'l bitch. This is shocking to me. Haven't you seen way badder hos out here in Dallas?" She held up my right arm and washed under it.

"Hell nall. Ain't nobody finer than my bitch. Besides, it ain't about all that. Me and Yani got history. We been through a lot. I need that girl. Don't nobody else understand me the way she do. I shouldn't have fucked up the way I did."

Carti smacked her lips. "Damn, you sound soft as fuck. On everything, I'ma need you to bring that Chi shit back out of you. I can't stand for a killer to sound like a rooty-poo-ass nigga. That's going to make me look at you hella different, and I don't wanna do that. You gon' roll wit' me tonight, and we gon' get the bitch-shit up off of you. It's a must that we do so. That sound like a plan?" She soaped up the towel and slid in under the water, grabbed my dick, and pulled him up before washing him and all between my legs.

"Shorty, if you disrespect me one more time, I'ma slap the taste out yo' mouth. Now, I get what you saying, so fall back. Get me clean so we can bounce. You dig me?"

"Aw, now you're tough all of the sudden? Nigga, please." She rolled her eyes and handled her bidness just like I told her to. "And yo' shit can quit getting all hard, 'cause ain't nothin' happening. Dang." She smiled and licked her lips.

No matter how angry I was, I couldn't stop my shit from rising. I was still healthy, and I was thankful for that. "Cuz, just get me right, and we'll worry about all of that other shit later."

She laughed and did what she had to do. I laid back while she did her thing, unable to get Yani off of my mind and wishing I'd never did to her what I had. I missed her so much.

To say I didn't feel somewhat better after the bath and sliding into some fresh clothes would have been a lie. Carti had copped me this black-and-red Gucci suit, along with the black-and-red retro #3 Jordans that had the Gucci logo all over them and the matching Gucci fitted cap. I felt like a young boss. I added the diamond studs to my earlobes, lotioned up real good, added some Gucci cologne, and stepped out of the house feeling a bit better than I had previously.

I guessed to coincide with me, she'd copped herself a tight-fitting Gucci dress that hugged her curves so right that I couldn't help but look at her. Her ass was poked out like a fat nigga's stomach. She had her makeup done all nice, and the black mascara enhanced her electric green eyes. She looked like a young, fly bossette.

She stepped off of the porch and walked around to the

driver's side of her Benz truck. The wind blew her hair. It waved around like a flag before she got into the whip and popped the locks.

An hour later we were sitting on the fifty-yard line watching the Saints and the Cowboys go at each other's throats in a close game. The stadium was packed. I tried to eat a few nachos, but every time my saliva mixed with the food I felt sick to my stomach, so I wound up eating a couple Hershey's and two Snickers. My body was craving that sugar. It wouldn't keep nothin' else down. I didn't know what was going on with me internally.

About midway through the second quarter, Carti turned to me and smiled. She was rocking a pair of Gucci shades with gold around the lenses. They made her look beyond a dime. Had I not grown up with her and known her like I did, I would have been mesmerized by her beauty, but I was familiar with it, so it had only a slight effect on me. She did look good, though.

"You enjoying yourself, li'l cuz?" She sucked some grape pop out of her straw.

"I'm good. I don't fuck wit' neither one of these teams, though. I'm a Bear, all day. Now that we got Khalil Mack, it's over wit'. That fool Tribisky balling, too."

Carti frowned. "Boy, I don't know what none of that meant. I don't know nothin' about football, period, but I wasn't about to turn down no free tickets. You saw the price tag on them jokers?"

I shook my head and scanned the audience, looking for any familiar faces. I ain't see none. I looked back over to her. She opened a bag of skittles and popped a few into her mouth, chewing. "Nall, I ain't peep 'em. Shid, I ain't have to pay for 'em. Besides, I would have never paid the sticker price fo' 'em, anyway, as racist as that punk Jerry is. He a straight slave master." I took a long sip from my pink Sprite. It had me feeling breezy. I was about fifteen minutes out from hitting my veins, though. The candy and lean could only do so much before I would need to handle my bidness with the North Korea.

Carti laughed. "Now you turning back into the asshole I'm familiar with. I like that shit. I don't be feeling when you be acting all soft and shit. Save that for your bitch." She snickered and nudged me with her shoulder after seeing I was ready to snap out on her ass. "Dang, boy, calm down. I'm just playing wit' you." She rolled her eyes and shook her head. "Hey, I'm here for you if you want to talk. You ain't gotta be this tough asshole all the time. I mean, we are family."

I looked out at the game and acted like I didn't hear her. She had me thinking about Yani again. I silently prayed she was okay, that she had come out of her coma. I just wanted to start from scratch with her. I was even considering allowing her to lead this time. I didn't know how long I would feel that way, but in the moment I was. I just missed her. I felt like a part of my heart was broken. A part of me was missing. I hated myself and was having a hard time being a part of me. "To be honest wit' you, Carti, after we leave here, I'ma need some of that pussy. I gotta take my mind off what I'm going through, and I already know one li'l bout in them guts'd do me a world of justice. Besides, it's long overdue. I ain't hit that cat since you was fourteen, and even then I ain't hit it like I wanted to."

She crossed her thighs, and that made the hem rise to show the underside of her right thigh. Damn, it looked good. Nice and juicy. I wanted to bite that muthafucka.

"Cuz, then I guess we on our forbidden shit tonight. I want some of you, too, especially if it's gon' help you come out of your funk. You too damn fine to be stressing like you are. You getting all skinny and shit. Don't worry, I'ma put this pussy on you and see what that do. I'm letting you know right now I ain't no li'l girl no more, though. This a grown-ass woman. Certified."

She took my hand and placed it on her thigh. It felt hot and soft as a pillow. I squeezed it. "Yeah, I'ma find out tonight, then. Matter fact, fuck Dallas and New Orleans. Let's get up out of here right now. I wanna see what that shit be about."

I got ready to stand up when she grabbed my wrist and pulled me back down. "Heinous, chill." She squinted her eyes and looked across the big football field.

I followed her gaze to see if I could see what had caught her attention. "What's good?" I asked, getting angry. I didn't like nobody grabbing all on me. I didn't care who they was.

She nodded her head. "If you look directly across the field, slightly to the right of the Cowboys' bench, you'll see Crescent sitting next to that nigga Killa. I wonder what they talking about. Did y'all ever squash that stuff from when he stole your truck and money when you first got down here?"

I was straining my eyes to locate them niggas. It took me a second, but I did, and as soon as I did, I felt my blood boil. I felt like running across the field and bucking that punk down. "Hell nall. I ain't been able to track him ever since I been down here. Crescent said when the time was right, we was gon' holler at him." I mugged both of them bitch-niggas. "I thought Crescent was supposed to be out of town until tomorrow night?"

"Me too, but clearly he ain't. Unless he considered Arlington as being out of town."

Something wasn't right. My gut was screaming out to me. I watched both of their mannerisms, and they seemed more than familiar with one another when I had been under the impression they were enemies. From the way they were laughing and joking with a bitch on each side of them, they looked as cool as a fan. Yeah, something was definitely out of whack. I would have to get to the bottom of that.

"Carti, text that nigga and ask him where he at. I just wanna see somethin'."

She pulled out her phone and did just that, sending him a one-liner.

Bruh, where you at?

From across the field, I could see him reach on his side and pick up his phone. He read the message, frowned, and texted her back.

Don't worry about it.

That was that. She exhaled. "That nigga don't never tell me what he be doing. You had a better chance of hitting him up than I did. Come on, let's get up out of here. I need some dick."

Chapter 11

Carti stepped out of the bathroom in a sheer purple Victoria's Secret robe that stopped just below her upper thighs. She wore a pair of red Christian Dior three-inch heels and had dropped her long hair so it fell down her back past her waist. She stood in front of the bathroom door, looking over at me. She'd painted her lips to match her pumps.

"Cuz, I might tell you to take it easy on me tonight, but trust and believe me when I tell you I don't mean it. I need you to dick me down. Can you do that?"

She opened the robe to reveal the black negligee underneath that had red trimming. The suit hugged her frame completely. Her breasts were pushed upward, exposing most of the globes. I could see a hint of her areolas. Her stomach was flat. A pink diamond belly button ring glistened in the lamp light of her bedroom. Her thick thighs were on full display, her knees slightly darker than the rest of her skin. Her legs were slightly bowed. She popped back on them and placed a tuft of hair behind her right ear.

I stood up and pulled my black wife-beater over my head. My dick was already growing in my boxers. "Yo, you ain't said nothing but a word. Bring that body over here, and let's get on with the show."

She dropped the robe on the floor. I met her halfway and grabbed her by the neck, slamming her up against the wall. She yelped. "Uh!" I put her arms above her head and sucked all over her long neck. I was finna tear her red pussy up. She tasted like vanilla.

"Damn, Heinous. You been waiting to fuck me, ain't you?" Her breathing was ragged. She squeezed her thighs together and moaned.

"I'm finna take this pussy like I wanted to do when we

were little. I got to. Bitch, you too bad." I picked her up and slammed her on the bed, stuck my hand between her legs, and rubbed her fat pussy through her panties. "Bitch, you already wet. You ready for li'l cuz to hit this shit, ain't you? Tell the truth." I dropped to my knees and opened her thighs wide, licked the material, and sucked some of her juice from it before licking up and down the satin, forcing it between her vagina's lips. Her left one popped out of the side and I trapped it, sucked hard, then ripped her panties off of her in one hard tug.

"Uh! Yes. Yes. Yes. Take it, nigga, damn!" She opened her thighs so wide I heard the bone in one of them pop.

I opened her wide, slurping, licking, flicking her clitoris. She humped into my mouth, shaking like crazy. "Un. Un. Un. Heinous. Eat this pussy, nigga. Eat me like you use to when we were little. Uh. You use to make me go back home and play wit' my li'l coochie all night, thinking about what you did to me. I wasn't ready for all that shit. I wasn't ready, cuz. Damn you."

I slid two fingers inside of her and ran them in and out while I sucked on her clit and ran my tongue up and down her crease before suckling her jewel again. Her cream oozed out of her and into my mouth. My fingers sped up. Her cat felt tight and slippery. "Cum for me, bitch. Cum all over my fingers before I bless you wit' this dick. You remember these fingers?"

"Uh! Fuck, yeah I do!" she screamed.

Back when we were twelve and she was scared to let me put my piece inside of her, all she'd let me do is finger her while I sucked on her titties that were just coming in. Her li'l kitty would get so wet. She'd be tossing and turning all over the bed. Her panties, which had a bunch of hearts on them, would be pulled down to her slim ankles. The room would smell just like her. I missed that shit.

I got to fingering her so hard and fast she brought her knees to her chest and came hard. "Ah! Shit! Heinous!" She fell back on the bed and screamed, scooted back, and started to finger herself. "Let me see your dick, cuz. Please. Let me just look at it like I'm a girl again."

Back when we were kids, we'd sit on the floor with our legs open and masturbate to the sight of each other's sexes until the both of us came. Then we'd go down on each other.

I stood up and dropped my boxers, kicked them to the wall, and stroked my piece in front of her while watching her fingers shoot in and out of her box. My shit jumped up and down in anticipation. Her fingers went deep into her crevice, faster and faster. I could hear the sound of her juices. They sounded so good to me.

"I'm finna cum again, Heinous. I'm finna cum! Aw, shit!" She fell backward, shaking like crazy and yelping. Her fingers got coated with her essence.

I crawled across the bed and licked all over her fingers, sucking the sides of her hand and all in her ass crack. I pushed her back and pressed her knees to her chest, busting her pussy wide open. I stuck my nose in it and inhaled hard like I did as a shorty.

She squeezed her breasts together and pulled on the nipples, moaning at the top of her lungs. "Fuck me, cuz! Fuck me! Please. Put yo' dick inside of me all the way or I'ma die." She sucked on her fingers.

I knelt beside her and pumped my dick, then laid my piece on her lips. "Suck me, Carti. Suck me hard. Hurry up so I can hit this pussy."

She swallowed me and got to doing her thing with no hesitation. The whole time she fingered her cat, moaning around my pipe. Her cat was pumping out thick traces of her essence. The cream highlighted the globes of her ass cheeks. I played with the cream, rubbed it all around and into her back door, slipped my finger into her rosebud before she got on all fours and really got to sucking me at full speed.

I reached over her shoulder and spanked that ass, squeezing the cheeks. I got to fingering her rose back there. "Yeah, cuz, g'on. Have to hit this ass, too, ma. Damn, you done got so thick. You ain't have none of this back then." I slapped it and squeezed it nice and hard. Some of the folds of her cheeks came in between my fingers.

Below, she sucked faster and faster. Her sucking sounds got louder. She added more spit. The tugging got more firm. It felt like she was using her hand instead of her mouth. I closed my eyes and groaned with my head tilted backward, my face toward the ceiling.

She popped me out if her mouth. "Uh, that's 'cause I wasn't a grown-ass woman back then. But I am now, and I'm as ready as I'm gon' ever be."

"Shut up, bitch, and handle this bidness." I grabbed a handful of her hair and slid back into her mouth, pumping my hips.

She took ahold of my pipe with her small fist and sucked me as if her life depended on it, faster and faster, gagging in between. That would cause her to slow her motions, then she'd speed right back up, giving me her all until I as on the brink of cumming harder than I ever had with her before. I got to imagining we were shorties again, hiding in the closet like back in the day while she acted all shy before sucking me until I came in her mouth. Oh, those had been the days.

She started to moan louder and louder. I kept fingering that ass, opening it up. Now two fingers had slipped inside of her. The heat pushed me over the edge. I tensed up and couldn't hold back. I grabbed her hair and forced her to take me deeper while I came hard, jerking into her lips.

"Mm. Mm. Mm," were the words she used while swallowing all of my contents, then she popped me out of her mouth and pumped it up and down with a tight fist. That brought a drip of semen to the top of my head before she licked it off.

"Damn, you still taste good, and I don't like the taste of nobody's nut." She sucked the head back into her mouth and took the pole to the bottom a few times before holding it and looking it over.

I was ready to hit that pussy now. I was tired of waiting. I needed to be inside of those walls. I picked her up and slammed her onto her back, got between her legs, and pulled them apart. I took my piece and trailed it up and down her thick sex lips, watching how they opened around the head. Her ooze came out of her center like a fountain, spilling over to the top of her ass crack. It looked so good with her cat all bald like that.

I pushed her knees to her chest. She reached around the side of herself and guided me into her hot hole. The lips peeled backward so she could accept me. I eased in inch-by-inch. It felt like a silk oven full of cushions. The deeper I slid, the hotter it got until my balls were resting against her fleshy ass cheeks.

"Uh. You're in me, cuz. You're in me. Shit, your dick so wide. So long. Okay. Okay. Now fuck me. Fuck me like we kids again, but on yo' grown man shit. Come on."

I situated her ankles on my shoulders and got to long-stroking that pussy while my fingers dug into the flesh of her thighs, pulling her to me so I could really dig into her womb harder and harder. She pulled me down and sucked my neck.

"Cuz. Cuz. Ooh. Fuck me. You fuckin' me. Harder, cuz. Harder. Uh. This yo' pussy. This yo' pussy. Uh. You finally back in me. Ooh. Shit!"

My hips were a blur. I'd pull all the way back and slam forward, crashing into her, hitting her soft bottom just to do it again. Every time I dug as deep as I could, she would scream in my ear and dig her nails into my back. Her juices came out of her as if she was peeing all over me. Her big breasts spilled out of her bra and danced up and down. The nipples stood up an inch from the mounds and begged to he sucked. The bed shook. The headboard banged at the wall as if it was driving in a nail.

"Uh. Uh. Uh. Heinous! You killing this pussy. Uh! Fuck me. Fuck me like you use to. Tell me this pussy better now. Tell me!" She bit into my neck, and her hands roamed all over my back. The nails threatened to leave scratches everywhere, but I didn't give a fuck.

"It tight. Yo' shit so wet. Fuck, you wet. Argh. Argh. Argh." I yanked her closer to me, sucked on her neck, and got to digging in her pussy as deep as I could, fuckin' her fast and hard. I could literally hear the sound of me going in and out of her. It sounded like a plunger trying to unstop a toilet, and she was just as wet. That pussy was forbidden and good. I was trying to wreck that shit. She was way too thick for me not to. Thick bitches deserved big dicks that murdered their slots. At least that's how I felt, and that's what I was giving her. That killer dick.

"Uh! Heinous! I'm cumming, cuz. I'm cumming. Aw, shit! Aw, shit, it's so good! Uh!"

I pushed her knees to her chest and got to hitting it at full speed, plunging and plunging as if I was trying to unstop her drain. There was a constant clapping sound from our middles connecting. Her pussy got to tightening around my length, milking me. I started to shake. I dug my nails into her thighs and came again, slamming into her with reckless abandon.

I laid on top of her for about two minutes, breathing hard. She slid from under me and laid me on my back, kissing all over my abs and up to my chest.

"I used to be obsessed with this body. Every time after we got done doing our thing and I'd go home with my parents, I'd get there and run straight into my bedroom, lock my door, lay on the bed, and finger myself thinking about you. Ooh, and in the tub was the best for me. I'd turn the faucet on as hot as I could stand it, then scoot under it and let the water run right into my li'l coochie, imagining it was you eating me or fingering me. You turned me out before I was even in the eighth grade. Dang, we use to do the most."

She stuck her hand between her legs and continued to kiss all over my stomach, then went lower and lower. She grabbed my dick and got to sucking her juices off it loudly. She'd deep throat it, stop, look up at me, smile, and then deep throat it again. Her electric green eyes peered into my own.

I sat back on the bed, my shit getting harder and harder. Her breasts rested on my thighs. I could feel the hard nipples poking me. They felt so good. Her titties were so perfectly shaped. They even hung just a little bit. That made them appear more real to me. I loved natural titties.

She popped me out of her mouth and straddled my waist, leaned all the way forward, and slid down on my dick with her eyes closed. She kissed my lips. "I'm riding you, cuz. You feel that hot-ass pussy? You gotta like that. This dick you putting in me. "Ooh. Ooh. Yes. Uh. Yes. Uh. Shit."

She sat all the way up and began bouncing up and down. I took ahold of her hips and allowed her cat to meow all over my shit. The constant tugging was indescribable. The sight of her titties dancing on her chest, flapping up and down was so hot that I pulled her close enough to me so I could suck them. I slobbered all over them pretty bitches like I was in heaven. I sucked on the big nipples, and pulled them just to watch them spring back to her mounds.

It felt like her pussy got wetter and wetter. She rode me faster and faster, slamming the headboard into the wall. I grabbed that big ass and forced her to go faster. Her titties snacked against her stomach.

"Cum, bitch. Cum. Cum all on yo' li'l cuz. Come on, bitch."

"Uh. Uh. Shut up. Shut up. Fuck."

"Cum on me, bitch. You know you twisted. You can't help that ho in you."

"Uh. Uh. Uh. Fuck you. Shit! Uh, fuck! I'm cumming! Damn, Heinous!"

She got to shaking so bad she fell off of me. She fell on her back with her legs wide open. The lips to her pussy were spread so far I could see her pink insides. I rubbed my thumb in circles all around her clit and made her cum hard, screaming at the top of her lungs again before I flipped her over and pulled her up on all fours. I got behind her and slid in deep, grabbed her hair, and pulled on her shit, making her arch her back.

"Damn, Heinous. You treating me. You treating me like a ho."

I slapped that ass hard, grabbed them hips, saddled up, and started to fuck her with all of my might. Long, hard strokes beat at her walls like a construction worker. Even I got to groaning under my breath a li'l bit, watching her ass ripple and jiggle. Carti had that A-1 pussy, and I knew I would be in it on a regular basis. I didn't give a fuck who she was fucking wit'.

She laid her face on the bed and started whimpering, rocking back and forth while I tamed that ass. "Aw. Aw. Aw. Aw. Aw. Shit. Aw. Aw. Heinous. Fuck."

Smack. Smack. Smack. Faster. Harder.

I pulled out and guided him into her back door slowly.

She opened her ass cheeks for me, whimpering louder. "Damn, nigga, get some if my pussy juices or somethin'. That shit too big for all of that."

She played in her kitty juices and rubbed them all around her rosebud, right where my head was inside of her body. I pulled him back, and allowed her to finish, then slid him back inside and went deep.

"Aw, shit! You gotta fuck me fast so I can get used to it. Fuck me fast, Heinous, please. Ooh-wee!"

I seized her waist and pulled her back into me, pushed her away, and pulled her back again. Over and over I repeated the process. Her hole felt so tight that it was like I was being suffocated. Her temperature was every bit of a hundred degrees, if not hotter.

There was nothing like fucking a bad, thick bitch, especially in the ass from the back. Carti was super bad. I had to enjoy that body in every hole I could fit.

Five minutes of full-speed fucking and it became too much. Her ass was crashing into my stomach, and her hole swallowed me whole. I got to piping her as fast as I could, listening to her screams.

"Aw! Aw! Heinous!" She diddled her clit and came hard at the same time I did. I knew because her anus got to squeezing me so hard I could barely move inside of her. I got to shaking like an earthquake, licking all over the back of her neck, sweat and all. Carti had that playground, and I felt like I was at recess.

When it was all said and done, she hugged up to me and threw her thick thigh across my waist, rubbing my chest. "Damn, I been fantasizing about what it'da be like to fuck you as an adult ever since I turned eighteen, and I gotta say, wow. Damn, these niggas don't be putting that pipe down like that down here in Texas. You needed to make some YouTube videos or something. I'll be the actress. I'm so, so serious." She kissed my neck and rubbed her finger across my cheek. "What you thinking about?"

I exhaled. "Yani."

She sat up and looked down on me. "Yeah, I figured that." She climbed out of the bed and stood on the side of it, naked. She picked up her robe from the floor. "I don't want this to be our last time, Heinous. I really enjoyed you tonight. You took me back to when I was twelve and all that shit. My body ain't felt that way in a long time. I –"

The door swung open and Crescent stepped into the room with his mouth wide open. "What the fuck y'all doing in here?"

Chapter 12

I slid into my boxers and threw my wife-beater back over my head.

Carti stood at the foot of the bed, naked, looking dumbfounded. "Dang, big bruh, whatever happened to you knocking?" she whined and slid her arms into her robe, tying the sash around her body. The material was so sheer I could make out her big nipples through it.

Crescent sniffed the air. "Y'all been fuckin'. I can smell that shit all in the air," he snapped.

"Nigga, if you think the air smell like something, you oughta get a whiff of my dick. No homo." I scoffed and walked past his soft ass, stood in front of Carti, and kissed her neck. "You got that sauce, shorty, fo' real. I'ma fuck wit' you later." I hugged her and stepped out of her room.

I wasn't more than twenty feet down the hall when I heard a loud-ass slap. Carti yelped, and then there was the sound of somebody falling to the floor.

"Bitch, you in here fuckin' this nigga? Yo' cousin? What the fuck is wrong wit' you?" Another slap.

"Stop hitting me, Crescent. It's just by marriage! Damn. Ain't no blood in us."

I rushed back down the hallway into the room and bumped his ass out of the way. "Nigga, get the fuck off of her. Don't be putting your filthy-ass hands on her. We grown."

He stepped into my face and pushed me so hard I fell over the bed. "Bitch-nigga! That's my li'l sister. Ain't no nigga gon' be up in this crib fuckin' her. I run this bitch. She under me."

I bounced up and jumped over the bed, cocked back, and punched him right in the mouth. I scooped him, carried him

127

into the hallway, and dumped him on his shit hard.

Wham! His back cracked. He rolled onto his side. "Aw, fuck! You bitch-nigga."

Carti ran out to get in between us. She had a red handprint on her face and blood in the corner of her mouth. "Please. Please. Y'all, stop this. Y'all, stop this. Please."

I pushed her ass out of the way and kicked this nigga as hard as I could in his ribs, flipping him over. "Nall, fuck that. This bitch-nigga ain't never supposed to put his hands on me. He rushing me and shit like he jealous that me and you doing our thing. Ain't no blood between us, you stupid-ass nigga." I kicked him again.

He rolled down the hallway a bit and winced in pain, holding his ribs, and curled up into a ball. I could hear him wheezing like he struggling to get air into his lungs. "Fuck," he muttered, barely above a whisper.

My temper was seething. I hated when a male touched me. The fact he'd pushed me over a bed and made me hit my head on the wall was enough to place me in a murderous zone. I didn't give a fuck if he was my cousin-in-law or not. He could've been my blood brother and I would have still got all in his ass like hemorrhoids.

I made my way toward him. Carti ran and jumped in front of me. "Please, Heinous. Please, don't fuck him up. You know that fool ain't 'bout that action like you are. He's just overprotective of me. I'm his little sister. I am begging you." She wrapped her arms around me and jumped on me, and the next thing I knew her legs were around me as well. Somewhere along the way her robe had fallen off of her body, so I had her naked ass trying to hold me back while Crescent struggled to get to his feet.

I slung her off of me. She hit the floor.

I got to him and looked down at him. "Fuck you tryna

do, nigga? We finna box, or what?" I was ready to bang this punk. I could still feel the spot on my chest where he'd pushed me, and that was pissing me off.

He was on all fours. He held up his hand. "My bad, nigga. Damn. Y'all just caught me off guard wit' that shit. I thought we was all family. That's all. I ain't know you was fucking her, that's all, cuz." He coughed and spit blood onto her white carpet.

"Yeah, well, we is. And it ain't none of yo' fuckin' bidness. Blood, on my moms, if you ever put yo' fuckin' hands on me again, on my word, I'ma knock that melon off of your shoulders. You gon' be around this bitch wit' just a neck. Don't no nigga touch me and live to tell about it."

Carti came and helped him up, wrapping her arm around the small of his back. I watched her titties bounce on her small frame. She looked up at him. "Boy, are you okay?"

He winced in pain again, holding his ribs. "Yeah. That nigga shouldn't be so fuckin' violent. Damn. We supposed to be family."

Carti rolled her eyes. "Says the nigga who just beat my ass because I wanted to fuck somebody in my room. You don't be tripping when you be bringing them hos home and wanting us to smash them together and shit, but if I wanna do my own thing, it's a problem. You know I don't need you to pay my bills, Crescent. I am more than capable. You can't keep treating me like a li'l-ass girl. I'm grown."

He stepped back and grabbed her by the neck so fast it shocked me. "Bitch, you belong to me. Don't be acting all funny in front of Heinous. I'll leave yo' ass standing. You know what it is. You hear me?"

She fell to her knees with him choking her. Tears came out of her eyes. "Okay. Okay. Ack! Okay."

He let her go and threw her naked-ass to the floor. She

scooted backward, got up, and ran down the hall to her room, closing the door loudly. "I'm tired of this shit! Tired of this fuckin' prison!"

I mugged Crescent. I wanted to smoke that nigga for what he'd just done. It always seemed like the softest niggas had a thing for beating women. I knew he couldn't fuck in my bidness on his best day. The occasional sobbing coming from Carti's room was fueling my rage.

He avoided eye contact with me. "I got a $50,000 lick for you, too. I'ma pay you out of pocket because I need two marks sliced up in a sadistic fashion. I need to make a statement to the streets." He waved me to follow him.

I stood there for a minute, wanting to go back and make sure Carti was okay. It appeared they had a strange relationship, but it wasn't my bidness. I'd fucked her, and I was gon' fuck her whenever I felt like it. That was all she could offer me. It wasn't my job to act like I was her man or somethin' because that wasn't the case. I was still just her cousin by marriage, and Crescent was her brother. Brother trumped cousin any day in my book, so I let that shit ride and followed him into the den where he had an ounce of North Korea on the table.

I rushed upstairs for my works, came back down, and got me a fix. I didn't give a fuck if I'd just exposed my habit to him or not. All of that fuckin' had dwindled my high, but after a few CCs of that raw, I was back, lifted like an elevator. I felt like a champion. "Speak, nigga."

He rolled up his sleeve and licked his thumb, rubbing it in a circular motion inside his inner forearm. He pulled a brand new syringe out of the table drawer and opened it, then used an alcohol pad to wipe the needles and his skin. He loaded the syringe with some of the North Korea and injected himself. I watched his eyes roll backward.

He smacked his lips, set the syringe on the table, and sat back. "I got a few niggas that ain't trying to play right. Niggas that's making shit real hard for me when it comes to my connection with Roman Velez. I need these fuck-boys sliced and diced. I know that's right up yo' alley, so I want you to handle this for me at twenty-five bands a head. Soon as you finish 'em, I'ma check yo' bag to you." He stood up and held his ribs. "Damn, you fucked me up."

I was so high he looked blurry to me. I had this song playing in my head that I had never heard before, but it made me angry. I didn't know what was going on wit' me. On top of that, I could have sworn I seen a dark figure standing in the corner of the room with red eyes and a hood pulled over its massive head.

"How soon you wanna handle this bidness? And I want twenty-five up front. You gon' quit dictating my paper. You know I'ma handle my bidness. What the fuck is a life to me?"

"I wanna handle this tomorrow night. I'm already setting everything up. That'll be the best time. Until then." He stepped out of the den and came back ten minutes later, tossing 250 hundred-dollar bills at me. "There you go. That's half. I'll have the rest for you when you finish the job. Cool?"

I thumbed through the money, glaring up at him. "When we gon' get up wit' that nigga Killa's glamour? It's been a few months now, and I wanna make that happen. So, what's good?"

Crescent ran his hand over his waves and shook his head. "I'm still working on that, but now ain't the time. I gotta conquer Roman Velez before he give somebody else uptown. These niggas standing in my way, so they gotta go. When the time is right I'll let you know. You got my word

131

on that."

I looked him over from the corner of my eyes and took a nice chunk of the dope on the table, brushing it onto the small mirror that was present, and prepared to take it upstairs. I stood up. "When was the last time you fucked wit' homeboy?"

He shrugged his shoulders. "I been looking around for that nigga, but he keep dodging me. I ain't seen him in a few weeks." He picked up his phone when it vibrated. "But don't worry about him right now. Just think about how you gon' fuck these twins over for me. That's what's most important. Besides, once I get ahold of uptown, you won't ever have to worry about no bread ever again. You got my word on that." He put the phone to his ear and waved me off before turning his back to me. "Yeah, what it do?"

I mugged him and lowered my eyes into slits. Now I knew something was most definitely up. I just didn't know what. This pussy-nigga had lied right to my face and didn't even stutter. Yeah, I had to keep him real close before he felt my inevitable wrath. Somebody was gon' pay me for the money I'd lost, and since it seemed as if he was canoodling with Killa, I was thinking it was gon' have to be the both of them.

***

Carti sat on the edge of her bed crying tears of pain when I knocked once on her door and then pushed it open. I'd just gotten out of the shower. She had changed into a pair of pink boy shorts and a pink wife-beater. Her long hair fell over her face. She looked like she was super stressed out and hurt.

I knelt by her side and looked up at her. "What's the matter, cuz? You still stressing over what that nigga did?"

She nodded. "I'm just tired of him. He think he's my man more than he is my brother. Some boundaries aren't meant to be crossed because ever since they was, my life has been a living hell. I wish I would have never let him buy me this house. I ain't need his help. I was more than capable." She covered her face and cried.

I ain't gon' lie and say I ain't feel no type of way, because I did. I knew Crescent was soft as a ripe banana. Ain't no way he would have done no man the way he had Carti. That was fuck-shit to me.

I kissed her knees, and then the inside if her thigh before getting up and putting my arm around her. "If you want me to smoke that nigga, I will. It wouldn't be no thang. Just walk up on this bitch and *boom boom*. Two to the head. You'd have to clean up the brains from the carpet, though, 'cause I ain't no janitor."

She laughed weakly, took a deep breath, and exhaled. "Damn, yo' ass crazy. You'd kill him for me for real if I asked you to?"

I nodded. "In case you don't know by now, I don't like your brother. Somethin' ain't right about his bitch-ass. I wouldn't have nothin' but a few bad dreams over his murder, if that."

No matter how much I hated a person when I killed them, I always knew I was in for at least two nights of cold-sweating nightmares. Whenever I took a life, that soul was going to haunt me before it passed on to the other side. That was just the way the game went.

I rubbed her back. "So, what's the word?

She sighed. "Nall, he still my brother. I wish I could because that seem like an easy fix. I'm so tired of him dictating my life. I just want to be free." She laid her head on my shoulder. "Heinous, if you left the game right now, do you know I could put you up on this real estate market thata have you seeing about a million dollars next year around this time? I also wanna partner my new club wit' you. I don't want Crescent's ass on the paperwork, he already locked in on enough stuff wit' me. But I might just do it myself. The city just always hollering this cosigner shit." She smirked up at me. "But all you know is the streets, huh?"

I stayed silent and held her closer to my body. "I can't think that far ahead right now. I just gotta make it out of this day. Tomorrow ain't promised to nobody. You feel me?"

She nodded. "Yeah, I do." She hugged me. "Heinous?"

"What's good, cuz?"

"Is it weird I wanna fuck wit' you beyond just this screwing shit?"

"What do you mean?"

She shrugged her shoulders. "Like, I really want you to be my nigga. I'm a go-getter, so you know you ain't gon' have to do much. I would be cool if you were around just to protect me. I really am tired of Crescent touching me, period. He won't let me fuck with no niggas, but he cool to let me have a bitch here and there. Ain't that some shit?"

I nodded. "That nigga gon' only do what you allow him to do. You should be able to fuck anybody you want to. That's your body, ma. He acting like he fucking you or something."

She tensed up and kept quiet. That told me all I needed to know. I mean, I couldn't confirm anything for sure, and I didn't wanna press forward. Crescent was a soft-ass nigga who probably got off on standing on Carti. She was bad, but he was still doing way too much if he was smashing her.

"Carti, on the low, you kinda always been my li'l dame. We was just real sneaky with it and didn't know what we were doing half the time. Now that we're grown, we're free to do whatever we wanna do. I'm fuckin' wit' you one hunnit percent, though. You can be my li'l one."

She smiled and stood up, straddled my lap, and kissed my lips. "I'm fo' real. I mean, I know you got a girl and all of that, but I want you, too. I'll help you get off of them streets and onto some corporate shit. You just gotta keep Crescent off of my back, and it's whatever wit' me."

She kissed my lips and pushed me all the way back, reached between us, and undid my pants. She pulled her panties to the side, sliding my dick into her wet hole again and riding me nice and fast. "Uh. Uh. Uh. He just mad. Uh! Uh. Uh. Uh. Mad 'cause he can't do me like this. Uh! Fuck, Heinous, yo' shit so big."

She rode me as fast as she could until I came deep within her channel. I didn't know where Crescent was, and I didn't give a fuck. His li'l sister's pussy was wrapped around my dick like a rope, and the more she moaned about how much he envied what he couldn't do to her, the better her pussy felt. She got wetter and wetter, too.

Before it was all said and done, we wound up fucking for a full hour. I curled up with her and fell asleep in her bed, spooning, my dick deep within the recesses of her cave. We slept the whole night through. Every time I woke up, if my dick had fallen out of her, I'd stroke my piece and put it back inside of her and fall back to sleep.

When I woke up the next morning, she was snuggled up under me wit' a smile on her face. She looked so damn good. I couldn't help but miss Yani, though. I wondered if she'd gotten better. The nurse had promised me they'd call when there was any kind of positive news to report to me, so I waited optimistically, terrified of checking in on her myself for fear of receiving the worst of the worst results. I knew I wouldn't be able to stomach that.

Hood Rich

Chapter 13

Crescent handed me a bottle of Ace of Spades the next night as we sat in the VIP section of Quest Nightclub. It was only eight in the afternoon, and the club wasn't set to open for another two hours, but he'd arranged to have a sit-down with the two studs he wanted me to hit for him. I didn't know why he preferred to meet them here, and I didn't care. I had half of my money, and I wanted the rest. I didn't give a fuck where I would have to handle my end of things as long as I was able too.

He sat a platter of North Korea on the table and separated it into thick lines, totaling twenty of them altogether. He kept a mug on his face as if he was the hardest nigga in the world.

"I don't like neither one of these clowns, Heinous. These fuck-boys think they're too big for their own britches. They been getting over on niggas in Dallas for a long time. One of the ways I'ma catapult myself to the top of the throne is to take these punks out, and what better way to do it than in the club they took from my father?" He smiled and frowned again.

I hit two of the lines to boost my high back through the roof. I started to hear the angry melody in my head again. I got to missing Yani and felt my depression try to resurface. I was still crazily worried about her, even though Carti had turned her charms up a whole three notches. Every time I looked up, she was under me, telling me how much she loved me and needed me. She couldn't keep her hands to herself. It was like the one taste of my dick had her going through it. I'd be lying if I said her pussy ain't have me feeling some type of way, too, because it did. Every time I smelled her perfume, I found myself rising like fumes in the air.

About ten minutes after we settled in, two heavyset,

pretty-boy-ass Mexicans came into the VIP section carrying their own bottles of Ace of Spades. They sat down across from me and Crescent.

The first one had long, wavy hair and a mouthful of diamonds. His facial hair was trimmed into a goatee. His eyebrows were lined, and his fingers were laced with a bunch of rings. He popped the cork on the bottle, and the fizz spilled over the top of it. "Well. Well. Well. Muthafuckin' Crescent. What brings you by the club, *vato*? you come to beg for us to give it back to your poppa? Oh, wait, that *vato's* dead." He snickered and turned the bottle up, swallowing nearly half of it.

The other one was less fat. He wore a pair of gold-rimmed Ray Bans. He had tats all over his face. He popped his cork and aimed it toward Crescent. The cork shot out and hit the bottom of the VIP couch right by his ankle, and he ain't say shit.

I had two Army serrated blades in the holsters of my fatigue jacket. I planned on cutting at least one of their throats out and tossing it into their laps. I didn't like them already, and murdering them would be like a walk in the park on a nice spring day for me. Easier than a promiscuous girl in high school.

The second one mugged Crescent, and then me. "Say, homes, who's this *vato* right here?"

Crescent glanced over at me. "This my cousin. He from out of town. It's all good."

The second one curled his upper lip, locking eyes with me. "You don't tell us when it's all good, homes. You brought him to us. We'll tell you when it's all good. You got that?"

Crescent nodded. "Yeah, that's my bad, bruh. But this my cousin, though."

The first one scooted to the edge of the couch. "Oh yeah? Well, what's your name, cousin?" He directed this question at me.

I sipped out of my bottle of Ace of Spades, burped, and wiped my mouth with the back of my hand. "My name Kiss My."

The second one scrunched his face. "Kiss My? What the fuck kind of name is that, *vato*? What's that, some of that African smack-my-tongue-just-to-talk-ass shit?" He started laughing.

I shrugged my shoulders and turned my bottle back up. "I guess so." Yeah, I was gon' enjoy sending them to the reaper.

The second one turned to Crescent. "What did you want to have a sit-down about, *vato*? We're here. Pay up the ten thousand for the meet-and-greet and we can proceed."

Crescent unzipped the small Gucci bag he carried and pulled out the money. "It's right here, bruh. It's all good."

The ten gees had a rubber band around it. After I stretched the two brothers out, I was gon' pick that cash up and add it to the fifty total I was getting for the job. That would bring me to sixty for the hit. That was good money. Back in Chicago, I would peel a nigga's cap for five gees, so this was a nice li'l come-up for me.

The first one counted the money in our face and slammed it on the table. "Speak, negro," he ordered.

Yeah, I couldn't wait to kill him. This punk had me itching all over my body. I was excited, and my heartbeat was more than irregular, waiting for the right moment.

"I wanna buy this club. I'll give you $200,000 cash for it tonight," Crescent said, sipping from his champagne.

They laughed in unison, the first one harder than the other. "That's peanuts. We can make $200,000 in a week in this location. That highway is everything. In and out, baby. No harm, no foul."

The second one slammed his champagne down, and the liquid went into the air and spilled all over the table. "So, that's your answer, nigger. Now, get the fuck out of here. Your time's up. You and this African weird-name over here." He nodded at me in disgust.

"$300,000, and I'll pay you ten percent of all wages earned for a year. Now, you can't beat that," Crescent tried, looking from one brother to the other.

The first one stood up. "The answer is no. Get the fuck out of our club before we turn your asses into *chorizos*." He grabbed Crescent by the shirt and yanked him to his feet. They tussled for a second.

The second brother came around to my side of the couch. "Get up, Kiss My. You gotta go, too. Both of you niggers gotta go." He reached down and took ahold of my left wrist.

I grabbed one of the Army knives out of my jacket and, with a swipe through the air, sliced him across the neck. I could literally feel the blade go into his skin and spread it. His blood skeeted into the air like a geyser. He slammed his hand over the wound, hollering and trying to stop it from spilling out of him, but it was of no use. It poured through his fingers and dripped off of his wrist. He staggered backward.

I stood up and slammed the blade into him eight quick times, then slashed him across the face four more times, dropping him to the floor. He flopped around like a fish, then stopped.

Crescent and the first brother were engaged in a wrestling match. The brother picked Crescent up and slammed him onto his back, then reached behind him to grab his gun out of the small of his back.

For a split second I thought about allowing him to blow Crescent's brains all over the club's floor. I even smiled in the midst of everything. But then again, I needed my other twenty-five gees. I didn't know where his stash was. If I had, I would have allowed the Mexican to body his ass.

I ran over and slammed the knife into the brother's neck, kneeing him in the side of the face. I pulled it out and looked down at him. He rolled over and hopped up, running with blood spilling from him at a rapid pace. He staggered and fell to his ass, scooted backward, and pulled his gun out, busting.

Boom. Boom. Boom. Boom.

I jumped behind the couch. Crescent fell to the floor and began to low-crawl. Now I was regretting not having brought a pistol to the fight.

The Mexican aimed and busted again. *Boom. Boom. Boom.*

"Argh!" Crescent hollered and grabbed his ass. He rolled behind the couch next to me, crying like a bitch. "I'm hit. I'm hit. Fuck, I'm hit."

I waved my hand over the top of the couch, and the Mexican started to bust again. He was busting one of those Remington nine millimeters. I knew from experience they only held thirteen rounds. I needed him to keep busting so I could finish my job. I didn't give a fuck about Crescent being shot. It was music to my ears when he bit the bait.

Boom. Boom. Boom. Boom. Boom. He stopped at twelve and tried to get back to his feet.

"Here I come, you pussy-ass Mexican!"

He turned around and busted. *Boom.* He fell to his chest, aimed back at me, and pulled on his trigger only to hear a bunch of clicking.

I was up and on his ass in no time. He tried to run, but

the blood loss got the best of him. He stumbled and crashed into a table in the lounge, right by the stage. I got there and tore his back up with stab after stab. I must've hit him thirteen times before I wrapped my forearm around his forehead and pulled his head back, slicing his throat from left to right and dropping him to the floor, where he bled out choking on his own plasma.

Before I left the club, I snatched up the ten thousand dollars and helped carry Crescent's bitch-ass out of there and back to his truck. More than once I thought about icing him. I was over this burden of a family member. Plus I ain't trust this punk as far as I could throw 'im.

***

Instead of Crescent going to urgent care to get his gunshot wounds addressed, he wound up having me drop him off at some nurse bitch's house he was fucking wit'. She was supposed to get the bullets removed from his ass and lower thigh. I don't know of she did or not because I booked it back to the crib, where Carti met me at the door and jumped into my arms.

"Baby, I been waiting on you all day long. I missed you so much." She kissed all over my face. "Come on, cuz, take me right now. I need some of you. I need some of you so bad."

I carried her ass into the hallway and fell against the wall with her. I could feel the handles of the knives pressing into my chest, hurting me. I needed to unsheathe them so I could knock her ass down. After a kill, some pussy sounded real good. Especially hers.

She licked all over my neck. "Mm, cuz. I need you."

"Wait, baby." I tried to balance her. My phone vibrated

in my left front pocket. I set her down and stepped back. Grabbing it out, I put it to my ear excitedly after looking at the screen and seeing it was the hospital. "Hello?"

"Sir, it's about Yaniece."

My heart dropped.

***

Yani sat up in the bed, staring at me with dark circles around her eyes. Her voice was hoarse. Her hair was all over the place. She looked like she was ten pounds lighter. Her skin looked darker. I could tell she was weak. There was still an IV in her left hand.

I stepped over to the bed and took her right hand. She snatched it away so swift it shocked me. "Don't touch me, Heinous. I fucking hate your guts. You did this to me. I'm lying here in this bed because of you." Her eyes misted over before the tears ran down her soft cheeks.

The machines beeped in the background. I couldn't even look at them, nor could I look her in her eyes. "Yani, I'm sorry, baby. I ain't mean to do what I did. I just couldn't stand the thought of you leaving me. You was flexing all hard on me and shit. I ain't never thought you'd come down on me like you did."

"So, then you did mean to do what you did."

"What?"

"Nigga." She started coughing. "You said you ain't mean to do what you did, but then you just gave me a reason for why you did it. That's contradicting your words. But you know what, Heinous? That's all you are: a walking, talking contradiction. You been that way our whole lives. It's all about you. If shit don't fit into your agenda, you'll find a way to force it to. You put poison into me twice. Not once, but twice. I'll never forgive you for this. I swear to God, I'ma get you back if it's the last thing I do."

I stood there feeling defeated. I didn't know what to say to her, and to be honest, there was nothing I could say. I had fucked her over not once, but two times. I had her lying in the hospital just avoiding death, according to the doctors. I felt like shit. "Yani what can I do? What can I do to make you forgive me? I mean, I fucked up, baby. I fucked up, and I know I did, but I don't want to lose you, Yani. I wanna let you lead now. I wanna follow you. Shit ain't been working with the way I been leading. I wanna trust you now."

She shook her head. "Nall. Fuck that. I fell for that shit before. I'm hip to that game. Nigga, you ain't who you say you are. You're a fuckin' clown. Only thing you're good at is death and destruction. You been that way since I met you. I thought I could change you. Silly fucking me. I swear, I wish I never met yo' ass. I'da been successful right now instead of lying in a hospital bed, fien'ing for some fuckin' China. Damn you!"

I don't know where they came from, but all of a sudden my eyes started to sting. I fought to keep the water from spilling out of them and rolling down my cheeks, but I couldn't help it. I don't think any man would have been able to. Yani was the love of my life. I didn't think I had loved any female in the world as much as I did her, and I didn't think I would ever be able to love in that same way again if her and I split indefinitely. In fact, my heart was cold because of the life I'd lived. I felt like she might've been the only person I really loved and cared about in the way I did. Second to her would have been Carti, but in my mind they were miles apart from each other. Yani and I had been through it all. We were meant to be together. I would change for her if she gave me the opportunity to, or at least I would have tried as hard as I could.

I wiped the tears from my face and took a step toward her. "Yani. Baby, please hear me out. I need you to know I'm –"

"Save it, Heinous. I don't wanna hear that shit. I already know where you're going with whatever you're about to say, and I just want you to save it for the next dummy, because I'm tired of your circus. I seen every act and been on every ride at your carnival of life. I'm sick of it. These people will be releasing me today into your care, and all I ask is you help me regain my strength and then let me go. I tried having them reach out to my immediate family, but thanks to me following you and burning the many bridges we did, I ain't got a pot to piss in. They don't want to have anything to do with me."

"Yani, I –"

"Will you help me regain my strength? Will you pick me up so I can spread my wings and fly like a butterfly? It's all I ask of you, Heinous."

The thought of allowing her to fly away like a butterfly literally made me sick to my stomach. I didn't know what losing Yani felt like. To not have her in my life for the rest of my life seemed like a death sentence for me. I knew I would never be able to let her go, but I was willing to tell her anything she wanted to hear as long as it would get her back under my care. "Baby, I'll do anything for you. Yes, I'll help get you back your strength, and when you're ready to go, I'll release you."

She glared at me. "You ruined my life, Heinous. Ain't nobody fuckin' wit' me because of you. Even though I don't trust you, I ain't got no choice other than to be released to you. Damn, this sucks."

I lowered my head and exhaled loudly. I felt like shit.

Hood Rich

Chapter 14

"Yani, just chill, damn. I ain't on shit," I snapped, taking the washcloth and dipping it inside the tub so I could wash in between her thighs. This was her first bath since she'd been released from the hospital, and she was giving me a hard time.

"I'm good, Heinous. You acting like I'm handicapped or something. I know how to wash my own ass, nigga, damn." She yanked the towel out of my hand and water popped into the air. Rolling her eyes, she pointed toward the bathroom door. "Bye, nigga."

"Dude, you still acting all funny and shit. When you gon' fall back and forgive me?" I asked, still sitting on the rim of the tub.

I ain't even think I had feelings until Yani got to hitting them bitches. It was like she was murdering each feeling one at a time. I figured out real fast how much I really loved her mean ass. I understood she had a reason for treating me like she was, but that shit still hurt worse than getting kicked in the nuts with steel-toe boots

She looked into my eyes and climbed partway out of the water until her forehead was up against mine. "Nigga, I will never fall back. You ruined my fucking life. All this time I thought it was me and you against the world and our enemies were those who looked to oppose us, but all along you've been my enemy. You've been the one trying to kill me, Heinous, so falling back ain't in the fuckin' cards. Now, get yo' crazy, stupid-looking ass up and get out of this bathroom. I don't need you to wash my ass. I got this."

She sat back in the water and threw her foot onto the side of the tub, slid the towel between her thighs, and moved it up and down under the bubbles. For some reason the sight of her doing that was so arousing I wanted to move those bubbles, stick my head under there, and eat her until she forgave me. I didn't care if it took all day and night.

"Bye, Heinous."

I stood up and flicked the water from my fingers into her face. "A'ight, well, fuck you, then. I ain't gon' keep kissing yo' ass, Yani." I stepped to the bathroom door and grabbed the handle.

She turned around and poked her naked ass up in the air. "Boy, if I told you to kiss my ass right now, you'd damn near break your neck to do it. Stop fronting. You know what it is. Later."

I stood there for a second, admiring the valley between her legs and imagining how it felt the last time I was able to hit that shit. Her cleft was nice and chunky, too. Her ass had a few stretch marks across it that made it look so fucking good to me.

She was right. If she told me to kiss her ass, I would have done it with no hesitation. I yearned to do it, but instead of submitting to her charms, I stepped into the hallway and slammed the door.

Carti was standing halfway down the hall. "Problems at home?" She snickered and held her arms open for me. "Aw, po' baby. You need a hug from mama?" she teased with a smirk on her face that showcased the deep dimple on her left cheek. She was dressed in a pair of real short Daisy Duke Prada denims that were all up in her gap. Her yellow thighs were heavily exposed. They looked like she'd just rubbed Baby oil into them. She crossed her arms in front of her chest.

Images of Yani's naked body came across my mind, so much so I felt myself getting aroused. I speed-walked toward Carti. "You know what? Hell yeah, I need a hug from mama."

I got to her, picked her li'l thick-ass up, and carried her down the hall into her bedroom. I kicked the door closed, threw her on the bed, and undid my pants.

She frowned at first, then smiled. "Oh, really? A'ight. I knew you wouldn't be able to stay away. It's cool. Come get this shit, then." She pulled her tank top over her head, and her perfect titties bounced on her chest.

I pulled her Daisy Dukes off her legs and threw them to the floor. She was without panties. Her kitty was freshly shaven. "I told you I was gon' hit this pussy whenever I wanted to. This me now. I don't give a fuck who in the house. Besides, shorty ain't fuckin' wit' me on that level no more, anyway."

I got between them hefty thighs, lined my piece up, and slid all the way in, filling her tunnel. She closed her eyes and moaned.

"Uh, Heinous. Damn, you so aggressive." She wrapped her legs around my waist and pulled me down to her while my hips were a blur, banging into her. Her pussy was so wet I could hear it already. It sounded like a person smacking on bubble gum as loud as they could into a microphone.

"Uh. Uh. Uh. Uh. Yes."

I bit into her neck. "Shut up, bitch. You being too loud." I pressed my lips to her and really got to hitting that pussy as hard as I could. My eyes were closed tight, imagining Yani's body, the soapy water all over her ass, and how her moon looked all shined up from the back. Yani was bad, and it was like now that I didn't have her any longer, I started to recognize that at every turn.

I forced Carti into a ball and really got to tearing that ass up, dicking her down harder and faster. I was so close to cumming already. I could feel it building in the pits of my stomach. "I'm close, shorty. I'm so close."

"Cum in me, Heinous. Aw, fuck, cum in me. This yo' pussy. This yo' pussy, cuz!" She dug her nails into my back and her teeth into my neck, cumming all over me.

My piece was like a battering ram. I was on her walls like graffiti, plunging and diving deeper and deeper. I imagined how Yani's pussy looked from the back, positioned right under her cheeks, and the imagery became too much. I came deep within Carti, squirting back-to-back. "Uh, fuck. This pussy so good," I groaned.

Carti was licking all over my neck when the door flew open and Yani busted inside the room in a bath towel with an angry scowl on her face. "Are you fucking kidding me? You're fuckin' Carti? This the reason I came out of my coma and yo' hype-ass wasn't nowhere to be found? It's because you were laying up with this bitch?" she growled and rushed the bed.

Carti pushed me out of the way and met her with a big bear hug. They tussled with one another, then fell to the floor. Carti was on top, trying to hold Yani's wrists.

"Calm yo' ass down, girl. We been fucking way before he even met you. Besides, he's my peoples. That ain't gon' stop y'all from doing whatever you wanna do with him." Her voice was strained.

"Let me up, bitch! Get off of me and fight me like a lioness. This some bullshit. You're fucking your cousin!"

"In-law, bitch. Only by marriage, and have been ever since I was twelve years old. This is old news. I don't want to fight you, Yani, so chill."

Yani leaned all the way forward and head-butted her against the cheek. She slung Carti off of her and began to rain blows into her face over and over. "Punk-ass bitch. Fuckin' my nigga while I'm in the hospital. I knew yo' li'l, pretty ass was trouble. Knew I couldn't trust you. Go fuckin' figure."

Carti rolled away from her and got up, threw up her guards, then hit Yani with three quick blows that left her woozy.

Yani swung at the air, punch-drunk. Her bath towel fell off of her body. She was as naked as Carti. Even under the circumstances, I couldn't help but admire both of their sexy bodies. Now that I saw both at the same time, they were neck-and-neck to me. I was upset and angry at the same time.

Carti grabbed Yani's hair and yanked her to the bed, slapping her across the face hard. "Bitch! For the record, I'm taking him. He my nigga now. I can do way more for him than you ca–"

Yani screamed and kneed her in the stomach. She took her foot, put it to Carti's waist, and catapulted her into the headboard before she rushed over and rained at least twenty hits all over her face. She we swinging so fast Carti got up and ran out of the room with Yani still clocking her ass again and again.

"Get that bitch out of my house, Heinous! She gotta go. She gotta go tonight," Carti yelled, running down the hall.

I stepped in front of the door and closed it, preventing Yani from chasing her. "Yo, chill, Yani. You won. The fight is over. Damn."

She rushed me and tried to pull me away from the door. "Get the fuck out of the way, Heinous, I'm serious. You know how it goes down in Chicago. When somebody getting they ass whooped, you stay out of it. Now, I was politely whooping that li'l, pretty bitch. Let me finish what I started. It's only right."

I shook my head. "Nall, baby, chill. That shit over wit'."

She hauled off and smacked me so hard I bent over with

my face feeling like it was on fire. My ears were ringing and everything.

Before I could say something, she smacked me again, then sat on the bed, screaming into her hands. "Ah. I can't believe you fucked my life over like this! You fucked me, Heinous. Oh, I swear to God, you ruined me so much!" She fell from the bed to her knees, crying and sobbing into her small hands.

I knelt down beside her. "Baby, please. I'm sorry."

She popped her head up and shot daggers at me. "Nigga, don't you ever call me baby again. I'll kill you if you do. Do you hear me? I will fucking kill you!"

***

Yani pulled the syringe out of her arm and sat it on the lamp table, wiped her nose, and closed her eyelids tight. She scooted all the way back on the bed while Jhené Aiko serenaded us through the speakers.

It was three hours later, and I'd finally gotten both her and Carti to calm down and forgive one another. They came to a conclusion they were not to blame. I was. Then they agreed both of them hated me mutually, and I would have to make a decision. Well, Carti called for a decision to be made. Yani still wasn't fuckin' wit' me.

"How do you feel, Yani? It's supposed to be the best of the best." I was walking a tightrope with her. I didn't want no more problems. I was so glad she and Carti had come to a conclusion without one of them demanding Yani would have to move out right away. That gave me some time to make up with her. I couldn't lose my baby. I loved her. She was the only female I loved as much as I did.

She smiled and opened her eyes just a tad. "I still hate

you. Ain't nothing gon' change that, but this shit is pretty fire. Every part of my body is tingling right now. I'm trapped, but free."

I was confused. "What do you mean?"

"Trapped because you've forced me back into this abyss and I don't want to be here, but I don't have any choice. And free because the North Korea has me floating on Aladdin's carpet. I wish I could stay here for the rest of my life. I hate what you've done to me, Heinous. I'll never forgive you. No matter what. I'll never forgive you for any of this." She smiled and closed her eyes. "Yeah, one of these days you're going to reap what you've sown. Only God knows when, though. But until that time, you're responsible for helping me regain my strength. My body is weak."

Once again she had me feeling like shit. As much as I didn't want to feed into it, it was so hard not to. Her and I had grown up together. I'd loved her ever since I was a mid-teenager, and she'd loved me. So, to hear her speak ill of me every time she opened her mouth was enough to bring me down into the dumps. But I knew I deserved the treatment, and no matter what it took, I was going to fight for Yani because I knew she was the woman for me. Even my mother, before she had fallen into the grips of heavy drug usage, had told me so. She'd always said Yani was my rib, that her and I were meant to be together, and I believed her. That truth became a part of my heart and one of the reasons I took to trapping her by use of the boy more than once.

"You know what, Yani? I know you hate me right now, and you can't stand the sight of me. But I swear I'm going to fight for you like crazy, because that's what you deserve. I know I done fucked up a whole lot, but I'ma get my mind right for you. I love you so much."

She opened her eyes and furrowed her brow. "Kiss my

ass, Heinous. I ain't buying that. You need to fight to talk to Jesus. Lord knows you need some spiritual healing. Talking 'bout you love me. Boy, bye."

Chapter 15

"This is what they call a lemon diamond tennis bracelet. You see, this bracelet gon' match the earrings I bought you, and this ring. You can either wear them as a set or at different times. Either way, they're yours." I set them on the dresser in front of her.

She eyed me angrily through the mirror inside the guest room. She'd just pulled her long hair back into a clean ponytail. She was without makeup. Her freckles were prominent. She looked pure and fine as hell in her natural state, dressed in a simple Nine West denim suit that hugged her every curve. Now that she had been out of the hospital for two months, she had gained back all of her weight. She was nice and thick again. Her face was even a bit more full. Her hair was growing again, and she had started to talk a lot more about what she wanted out of the future. Whenever she got to doing that, it made me feel low because I could tell she didn't see me in it.

"Heinous, you can buy me all of the shit in the world, it still ain't gon' make up for what you did to me. I don't know why you can't get it through your head, but I ain't fuckin' wit' you no more. You can forget about that. Everything that glitters ain't gold." She added some hoop earrings to her earlobes and picked up the jewelry I'd sat in front of her. "This is nice, though. You did a real good job for once." She continued to look it over with admiring eyes, then tossed it over her shoulder and onto the floor. "I can buy my own jewelry. I'm a boss, through-and-through. Today is going to be a great day. I can feel it." She added a li'l gel to her edges, then stroked them with a small brush.

I picked up the jewelry and placed it back inside its boxes before dropping it into the jewelry bag it had come inside.

"Yo, so I guess you gon' act like a stuck-up bitch for the rest of our time together, then?"

She scrunched up her face and then turned around to face me. "Oh, so you thought you was gon' buy me some $10,000-ass jewelry that I can buy for myself and everything was going to be all good between us? Huh? Nigga, you forget I got my own money. If I want some jewelry, I'll go out and buy it for myself. I ain't one if them bum bitches you're used to dealing with. I can make it happen for myself. Now, the only reason I'm going out with you tonight is because I'm tired of being in this house, and I don't trust myself to drive somewhere on my own just yet." She curled her lip. "And I ain't acting stuck-up, nigga. I been stuck up. You ain't notice it because my walls were down for your punk-ass. But now they're up like the great ones in China." She rolled her eyes.

I was about to go in on her when there was a knock on the guest room door. I opened it, and there stood Carti giving me the 'come here' signal with her forefinger. "Let me talk to you for a minute, Heinous."

I mugged Yani one last time and snatched up the bag of jewelry before stepping into the hallway and closing the door behind me. "What's good, Carti?" I sounded defeated and weak. My brain was spinning and trying to find ways to get Yani back. I was running out of ideas, but I didn't want to give up. I think the more she turned me down, the more I wanted her.

Carti grabbed my wrist and pulled me away from the guest bedroom door. "Heinous, why you keep letting that bitch talk to you like that? She treating you like shit. That look real bad, li'l cuz." We stepped into her bedroom, and she closed the door once I came in and sat on the edge of her bed.

"That's my baby, Carti. We done been through a lot of shit together. I done fucked her over in more ways than you can ever understand. I gotta fight for her. It's my fault she acting this way."

Carti jerked her head backward. "Your baby? Then what the fuck am I?"

I exhaled hard. "Man, come on, I don't need this bullshit right now. You know what I meant."

"No, I don't, which is why I am asking you. If she is your baby, then what am I to you?" She came and stood in front of me, right between my legs, with her arms crossed.

I stood up and wrapped her in my embrace, holding her tight. I couldn't stand to lose her security just yet. I still needed a place to lay my head until I could come up on at least twenty more gees. I needed to say and do whatever I had to in order to keep her within my grasp. We had already went nearly a month without screwing so far because I was worried about Yani catching us in the act again. I just didn't need any more division between Yani and myself, but I could tell me not screwing Carti was getting the better of her.

I kissed her lips and sucked on them hard. "You're my heart. I'm crazy about you. There is a big difference. You gotta know that."

She accepted my affection, then pushed at my chest. "Yeah right, Heinous. That bitch got you wrapped around her little finger. Every time I just watch you and see the way you're peeping her when you're in the same room with her, it just gives me clarity. You're in love with her. I mean, that real mad love, too. That love most women dream about. I know you don't really care about me, and if you do, it ain't got shit on the love you have for her. And that sucks because I can do a lot more for you than she ever could. I actually care about your nutty ass a great deal. My love is unconditional. You ain't gotta buy it like you're trying to do hers. But that ain't the reason I asked to speak with you." She stepped to her dresser and opened the top drawer. "You're going to have to make a decision, and fast, because I ain't gon' keep going back and forth with this bullshit. I ain't been feeling right for a nice amount of time now. And, well, here." She unwrapped a pink towel she'd taken out of the drawer and pulled two pregnancy tests out of it, handing them to me. "I'm pregnant. You're the father. What are we goin' to do?"

I took the tests and stared down at them, awestruck. "Carti, are you serious? You're pregnant? When? I mean, we ain't fucked in almost a month. When did you find out?"

"Like I said, I been feeling real foul for a minute now. I took these pregnancy tests two weeks ago, and I was gon' say something to you about it, but I decided not to. I didn't know what I was going to do at first, and I still don't. I wanted to let you know so we can figure that out together. I wanna have this baby, and I wanna be with you. How do you feel?"

I lowered my head and looked down at the pregnancy tests again. "Damn, ma. I ain't even expect this. I mean, a baby? Right now? Damn, it's so much shit I gotta get in order before I can call myself somebody's father. I mean, I love you and all, and you'd be the best baby mother for me, but baby, I gotta get my shit together first. Seriously."

She stepped forward and smacked me so hard I spit a li'l bit. I held my face and balled my fists.

"Nigga, what the fuck did you think you cumming in me was going to do? Huh? It's common fuckin' sense, Heinous. If you cum in me, there's a high probability I'm going to get pregnant. Now you're telling me you aren't even ready to be a father? Are you out of your fuckin' mind?"

Yani opened the door with a serious mug on her face. "You got this bitch pregnant? She's about to have your child? Really, Heinous?"

I looked back and forth from one female to the other, speechless. I stated to address what Yani had just said, but Carti stepped in my face.

"What are you going to do, Heinous? I want to have this baby, and I need you there as well. I can't do this on my own. Well, I could, but I don't want to. I need to know if you're going to be a man and step up to the plate."

Yani pushed her out of the way. "Move, bitch. Y'all can do that shit later. This nigga owe me a night out on the town, so that's what I'm about to get. Whatever y'all gotta figure out, that shit can wait until later. Let's go, Heinous."

Carti bumped into the dresser and gathered herself. She caught her balance and balled her fists. "I'm so tired of this punk-bitch! Trick, I let you stay in my house rent-free. I don't bother you. I am very respectful toward you, and all you do is cause chaos. I want you out of my house by tomorrow night. I can't take this shit no more. Pack your shit and go. Heinous, if this who you gon' be with, then so be it. You know my condition, and I've said what I said. Holler at me as soon as possible."

Yani mugged her. "Bitch, I should beat that baby out of you, but you know what? I ain't gon' be petty like that. I'ma leave your house like you asked me to, but it ain't gon' be tomorrow. It'll be Monday. Far as you and Heinous go, I hope y'all live happily ever after." She bumped me out of the way and shot out of the door.

Carti shook her head. "I hate that bitch." She turned to me and looked into my eyes with her green ones. "So, what you gon' do, Heinous?"

I took a deep breath and shook my head. "I'ma handle

my bidness like a man. I gotta make sure you are –"

Crescent rushed into the room with a pistol in his hand. "Heinous, come on, man. I need to holler at you right now. It's urgent! His face was covered in sweat. He looked bewildered. His eyes were bucked wide open.

Chapter 16

"Remember I told you we was gon' holler at that nigga Killa when the time as right? Well, the time is right. We about to go holler at him right now and make worm food of his punk-ass," Crescent said, treating his nose.

Instead of us running out of the house to go and handle our bidness, he decided to take a pit stop in the den so he could get his system right with that North Korea. He had me so confused because that wasn't how we got down in Chicago. All that dope, fun, and games waited until after the beef was done. Once the adversaries were annihilated, then it was time for kicking back. Not before.

I looked across the table at him with a mug on my face. I was irritated because of what had taken place between Yani, Carti, and myself. Then he'd busted into the room, making it seem like it was an emergency, but now here we were, sitting in the den and getting lifted when I felt we should've been in the streets handling bidness. "Nigga, you rushed into the room like there was some kind of an emergency, got me all hyped up, only to bring yo' ass in here so you could come and sit down? What's really good?"

My nostrils flared, and I could feel my blood pressure rising. I was low-key stressing over the girls. Yani was insisting on me taking her out. She acted like she didn't care about the fact Carti was pregnant, and that was bothering me because it was like she had fully let me go emotionally. That was crushing my whole soul. I wanted to get things right with her, and I also wanted to get an understanding with Carti. I didn't want her to think I wasn't gon' handle my bidness for her, because that trifling-nigga shit wasn't in me. There was no way I was gonna turn my back on her and my child, but at the same time I didn't want to lose Yani, either.

I was hoping our night out would allow us to get an understanding with each other.

"Cuz, we definitely about to handle bidness, but I ain't had none of my shit in my system all day. I was feeling sick. So, once I get right, my head will be clear and we can move the way we need to. Besides, that fool laid up with two of my Brazilian bitches at my trap over on McKinney. He think it's good. He ain't going nowhere for a minute. We got time. Trust me on that. I let one of the bitches roll my whip, so we gon' have to jump in my trapper to handle this bidness. It's long overdue, I already know, but trust me when I tell you it was worth the wait. I just had to make sure everything was in place before I moved. Now that it is, we're good." He pushed the platter away and got out his works. "That nose ain't working for me. I need to get right-right, you know what I'm saying?"

He smiled, and for the first time I noticed he was sitting sideways on the sofa. I was guessing that bullet to his ass was still messing with him real bad. "Why was it worth the wait? And what's in this shit for you? I know you don't do shit unless you got a stake in the proper outcome."

"I just want you to knock his head off. Get your revenge. In doing so, that'll move him out of my way. When we hit that nigga tonight, he gon' have 2.5 million dollars in cash on him, then forty bricks of the North Korea in his trunk. I know them bitches there because I packaged and loaded them myself. He suppose to be dropping the bricks off in Phoenix, and the money goes to Roman Velez. But it ain't gon' get there, if you get my drift. You and I gon' split the money down the middle. We gon' do the same with the North Korea. That's twenty apiece. How does that sound?" He smiled as he injected himself with the poison, smacking his lips loudly.

"It sound like I won't believe that shit until I see it. What time are you trying to do this, anyway? Because I got other bidness to take care of."

"Three hours, li'l cuz. Three hours and we should be good to go. So, go handle yo' bidness, and by the time you get back, we should be good."

***

Yani walked along the rocks of the lakeshore and stopped. She hung her head before looking out at the water as the wind blew violently. Her clothes flapped. Her long hair blew, as well. She pulled her Chanel leather jacket tighter around her and adjusted her earmuffs, took a deep breath, then began to climb the rocks, not stopping until she got to the top of the pile. Once there, she sat down and continued to stare at the sun as it set behind the water.

I climbed the rocks, following her path. My Jordans gripped the slippery surface of them just barely. I didn't know how she'd managed to climb them in a pair of Steven Madden's, but she had.

When I got to the top, I sat beside her and tried my best to collect my thoughts. I wanted to say so much to her, but my brain kept on drawing a bunch of blanks. All I knew was I loved her and wanted to say the right words so I could keep my baby. I didn't know how possible it was, but I was willing to try.

The sun slowly lowered itself, casting an orange glow over the rippling water. There was a small boat off in the distance. The blue flag on it waved over and over. The wind appeared to be more harsh than it was twenty minutes prior. It also smelled like rain was coming.

"How did we get here, Heinous?"

The bit of sunlight that was left shone off of her big, juicy lips. She smelled so amazing. Her scent sent chills through me. I missed Yani. Not physically, but soulfully. I missed her spirit. Our connection. Her love for me.

"Baby, I just love you so much, and I never wanted you to leave me. I know I was bogus for injecting you with that shit, but it was only because I didn't want you to go. You're always talking about all of these plans that don't involve me, so I got on some sucka-shit. I'll never forgive myself for turning you out, but what's done is done."

She was quiet for a second, then smacked her lips. "That's what's wrong wit' niggas from the hood. Or men, period. Anytime a woman get to talking about accomplishing her dreams, y'all wanna find a way to pull us down. That don't make no sense. You ever stop to think I could have been your ticket out of the slums? That because of my ambition, I could have gotten the both of us out of the hood? Damn. Not once have I though about being successful and leaving you behind, Heinous. I love you just as much as you love me. Always have. And even though you're tricking, I always will." She shook her head. "But we can never be together, though. Not after all you've put me through, and not after you getting your cousin pregnant. I legit hate that bitch. Like, legit, pure-ass hate. That bitch moved in on you while I was in the hospital. That's just trifling."

"I fucked up, baby, but I'm not about to let you leave me like that. I love you way too much. I'll do anything for a second chance. I just need to show you how much I care about you. I been fucking up my whole life, but you're the one and only thing I've ever done right. When I look at this cold, cold world, I have thoughts of giving up on life every single day. Just getting on some kamikaze shit and going out like an animal. But because you're here in this world, you give me a reason to keep on fighting. This shit is serious, baby. If I ain't got you, then I want the reaper to come and see me ASAP. I've been in love wit' you since day one."

She remained quiet, but after about two minutes looked over to me with tears in her eyes. "You got her pregnant, Heinous. You got another bitch pregnant while I was at my lowest point. A point you drove me to. You actually fucking injected me, sent me to the hospital, then jumped between this bitch's legs. I was literally fighting for my life in the hospital bed, alone. Instead of you being by my side, you were too busy planting your seed in that bitch who don't love you half as much as I do. I would have died for you, Heinous. I would have fucking died for you with no hesitation. None. But now, with all of this shit that happened since we been in Dallas, coupled with our Chicago Drake? Man, Heinous, you're toxic. I love you, and I hate how much I really do, but all I can offer you is a fresh start. A friendship." She broke into a sobbing fit. "I love you so much, and I don't want to lose you to that Carti bitch, but I'm tired. I'm so fuckin' tired."

I snatched her into my embrace and held her. "You will never lose me, baby. Never. I love you with all of my soul. I need you. You gotta give me another chance. I'll do whatever it takes." The tears spilled from my eyes and ran down my cheeks before the cold wind dried and stained them on my face. I held her and felt my soul draining out of me. I was willing to die for this woman.

She shook her head. "You hurt me too bad, Heinous. You hurt me too, too bad. I love you, Heinous. I swear to God I do. I'm so confused."

***

When we pulled back up to the house, Crescent ran to the truck and jumped in the back of it. "Yo, my trapper won't start. Yani, you gotta let us use this whip, because we gotta meet somebody somewhere right now. We're already late."

"Nigga, you done lost your mind. You think I'm about to let you roll my BMW, you got another thing coming. I'm finna mark my shit. Get out, Heinous."

"Man, holler at yo' bitch, li'l cuz. She tripping," Crescent snapped, hitting the back of my headrest.

"You's a bitch-nigga. You don't know me like that to be calling me all out of my name. You better check yourself before I get all in your ass like a wedgie. Heinous, holler at yo' peoples, fo' real."

I looked back at him. "Be cool, bruh. You shouldn't have gave your whip to that Brazilian broad. Now it's finna cost us ten gees just to have Yani drop us off."

"Ten gees? Aw, hell yeah, I'll take ya wherever you wanna go." She pulled from in front of the crib and made her way down the street. "So, where we headed?"

Crescent exhaled and shook his head. "Damn, she taxing like a muthafucka. We better off taking a Uber."

"Nall, nigga, it's to late. I'm driving. I'll take my shit in cash. Chi town in the building," she laughed.

"Man, it is what it is. We headed to McKinney Avenue. I'll direct you the whole way," Crescent said, sitting back in his seat, defeated. He pulled out a knot of hundreds and handed them over her seat to her.

Yani snatched it. "Pay me, nigga. That's what I'm talking about."

***

Crescent placed his hand against my chest as we crept up

the back steps of the McKinney Trap and stopped right at the back door. He placed his hand on the knob. He had his Glock in his right hand. We'd already walked past his truck that had been parked in the back yard, along with a Range Rover he said belonged to Killa. That told me his bitch-ass was present.

"They gon' be right in the living room, having a threesome on the floor. The money gon' be in the back room off of the kitchen. Dead that nigga, and I'ma go for the money. Don't hit shorty an' 'em. I'ma take care of they ass later. Just focus on Killa. You ready?"

I had twin forties out, one in each hand. I was more than ready to go, and I wasn't buying that shit about letting the two hoez live. I felt like they were links back to me, I would have to play that whole situation by ear. "Nigga, let's go, just don't get in my way."

He nodded and tossed open the door. I ran right into the house. It smelled like pussy and loud, and all I heard was a bunch of moaning and groaning like somebody was getting killed. All of the lights were out, and the closer I got to the living room, the louder the moans got. I could see the flickering of candles.

I rushed right up to the bedroom through the living room, looked at the bed full entangled flesh and aimed at the big nigga on top of one of the Brazilian girls, jumping away like his life depended on it. "Say, Killa!"

He stopped humping and looked over his shoulder with sweat all over his face. "Aw, you muthafucka. Crescent, you —"

Boom. Boom. Boom. Boom.

"Ah!" screamed one of the Brazilians. She scooted from under the fallen Killa. His brain matter was spattered all over her face. There were chunks of meat stuck in her curly hair.

Her face looked like she'd dunked it inside a big bowl of spaghetti sauce.

Her friend got up from the bed and tried to run out of the room when Crescent raised his banger and busted twice, knocking her into the kitchen. She struggled to get up, then fell back on her chest. A big puddle of blood appeared under her. I didn't understand why he shot at them, being that he told me not to. It had to be personal. I wouldn't stand in the way of their personal affairs.

The first Brazilian got up and ran into Crescent's arms. "Please. Please, baby. Don't do me like you did her. I've done my part. I did everything you told me to do," she pleaded.

He pushed her off of him and hit her with two, both through the forehead. She twisted and fell on her side, both legs kicking wildly. There was a high-pitched screeching emitting from her throat before she faded away.

"Come on, Bruh. The money in here." He rushed into the back room and knocked over a big dresser, kicking a hole in the wall. The drywall sunk in easily. Once it did, he moved a bunch of the plaster and pulled out one duffle bag at a time. They were all black with some of the drywall spilled on top of them. "That's the North Korea, bruh. And this is the money, right here." He stuck half of his body inside the big hole and pulled my suitcase out of it, dropping it in front of me. "Grab the work. I'll grab the money." He picked the suitcase back up and got ready to run out of the room.

I grabbed his arm. "Hold on, nigga. We can split this North Korea, but we ain't splitting this." I yanked the suitcase out of his hand and opened it up. Sure enough, it was my cash. I recognized the rubber bands with the red ink stains on them.

Crescent cursed under his breath. "I knew this shit was

gon' happen."

He upped his gun and aimed, firing twice, catching me in the chest. I flew into the wall and slid down it. The bullets felt like hot coals burning through my system. They cut off my breathing.

Crescent stepped over me with a grin. "Pussy-ass nigga. You ain't hard now, is you? Fight me now, nigga. Aw, you can't 'cause you bleeding out." He kicked me in the ribs. "Payback a bitch, ain't it?"

I rolled onto my side and struggled to get back to a sitting position. He bent down to pick up all of the bags. I raised my Glock and finger-fucked the trigger over and over again, giving him all neck and side-facials.

He fell forehead-first to the ground while I struggled to breathe.

***

I dragged the suitcase of money across the back yard, wheezing. Blood poured out of me at a rapid pace.

When I made it to the alley, Yani saw me and jumped out of the truck. "Oh my God, Heinous!" She ran to me at full speed and stopped in front of me after seeing my condition.

I could barely breathe. "Yani, take this money. It's yours, ma. It's yours. Live your life." My chest felt like it was being ripped apart. My lungs were on fire. I started to cough up blood and collapsed to the ground.

She took me in her arms and broke into tears. "Why, Heinous? Why? Why couldn't you let me lead? What am I goin' to do without you? It's always been us!"

Sirens rang in the distance. I tried to tell her how sorry I was, but no words came out. Only more blood. The coughing started, and the reaper appeared ten feet away from us in a dark hood, its eyes the color of burning emeralds.

The sirens got closer.

Yani kissed my lips and jumped up. "I love you, Heinous. I'ma do my thing for us. You'll see you should've followed me."

She grabbed the suitcase, got in her truck, and smashed away.

To Be Continued...
Kingpin Killaz 4
Coming Soon

Submission Guideline

Submit the first three chapters of your completed manuscript to ldpsubmissions@gmail.com, subject line: Your book's title. The manuscript must be in a .doc file and sent as an attachment. Document should be in Times New Roman, double spaced and in size 12 font. Also, provide your synopsis and full contact information. If sending multiple submissions, they must each be in a separate email.

Have a story but no way to send it electronically? You can still submit to LDP/Ca$h Presents. Send in the first three chapters, written or typed, of your completed manuscript to:

LDP: Submissions Dept
Po Box 870494
Mesquite, Tx 75187

DO NOT send original manuscript. Must be a duplicate.

Provide your synopsis and a cover letter containing your full contact information.

Thanks for considering LDP and Ca$h Presents.

Hood Rich

BOW DOWN TO MY GANGSTA

By **Ca$h**

TORN BETWEEN TWO

By **Coffee**

BLOOD STAINS OF A SHOTTA **III**

By **Jamaica**

STEADY MOBBIN **III**

By **Marcellus Allen**

BLOOD OF A BOSS **V**

By **Askari**

LOYAL TO THE GAME **IV**

LIFE OF SIN II

By **T.J. & Jelissa**

A DOPEBOY'S PRAYER II

By **Eddie "Wolf" Lee**

IF LOVING YOU IS WRONG… **III**

LOVE ME EVEN WHEN IT HURTS **II**

By **Jelissa**

TRUE SAVAGE **VII**

By **Chris Green**

BLAST FOR ME **III**

A BRONX TALE III

DUFFLE BAG CARTEL III

By **Ghost**

ADDICTIED TO THE DRAMA **III**

Kingpin Killaz 3

By **Jamila Mathis**

LIPSTICK KILLAH **III**

Mimi

WHAT BAD BITCHES DO **III**

A HUSTLER'S DECEIT 3

KILL ZONE **II**

By **Aryanna**

THE COST OF LOYALTY **III**

By **Kweli**

SHE FELL IN LOVE WITH A REAL ONE **II**

By **Tamara Butler**

RENEGADE BOYS **III**

By **Meesha**

CORRUPTED BY A GANGSTA **IV**

By **Destiny Skai**

A GANGSTER'S CODE **III**

By **J-Blunt**

KING OF NEW YORK IV

RISE TO POWER III

By **T.J. Edwards**

GORILLAZ IN THE BAY III

De'Kari

THE STREETS ARE CALLING II

Duquie Wilson

KINGPIN KILLAZ IV

STREET KINGS 2

Hood Rich

STEADY MOBBIN' **III**
Marcellus Allen
SINS OF A HUSTLA II
ASAD
TRIGGADALE II
Elijah R. Freeman
MARRIED TO A BOSS II
By Destiny Skai & Chris Green
KINGS OF THE GAME II
Playa Ray

<u>**Available Now**</u>
<u>RESTRAINING ORDER</u> **I & II**
By **CA$H & Coffee**
<u>LOVE KNOWS NO BOUNDARIES</u> **I II & III**
By **Coffee**
<u>RAISED AS A GOON I, II, III & IV</u>
<u>BRED BY THE SLUMS I, II, III</u>
<u>BLAST FOR ME I & II</u>
<u>ROTTEN TO THE CORE I III</u>
<u>A BRONX TALE I, II</u>
<u>DUFFEL BAG CARTEL I II</u>
By **Ghost**
<u>LAY IT DOWN</u> **I & II**
<u>LAST OF A DYING BREED</u>
<u>BLOOD STAINS OF A SHOTTA I & II</u>

By **Jamaica**
LOYAL TO THE GAME
LOYAL TO THE GAME II
LOYAL TO THE GAME III
LIFE OF SIN
By **TJ & Jelissa**
BLOODY COMMAS I & II
SKI MASK CARTEL I II & III
KING OF NEW YORK I II,III
RISE TO POWER I II
By **T.J. Edwards**
IF LOVING HIM IS WRONG…I & II
LOVE ME EVEN WHEN IT HURTS
By **Jelissa**
WHEN THE STREETS CLAP BACK I & II III
By **Jibril Williams**
A DISTINGUISHED THUG STOLE MY HEART I II & III
LOVE SHOULDN'T HURT I II III
RENEGADE BOYS I & II
By **Meesha**
A GANGSTER'S CODE I &, II III
By **J-Blunt**
PUSH IT TO THE LIMIT
By **Bre' Hayes**
BLOOD OF A BOSS **I, II, III & IV**
By **Askari**
THE STREETS BLEED MURDER **I, II & III**

Hood Rich

THE HEART OF A GANGSTA I II& III
By **Jerry Jackson**
CUM FOR ME
CUM FOR ME 2
CUM FOR ME 3
CUM FOR ME 4
An **LDP Erotica Collaboration**
BRIDE OF A HUSTLA **I II & II**
THE FETTI GIRLS **I, II& III**
CORRUPTED BY A GANGSTA I, II & III
By **Destiny Skai**
WHEN A GOOD GIRL GOES BAD
By **Adrienne**
THE COST OF LOYALTY
By Kweli
A GANGSTER'S REVENGE **I II III & IV**
THE BOSS MAN'S DAUGHTERS
THE BOSS MAN'S DAUGHTERS II
THE BOSSMAN'S DAUGHTERS III
THE BOSSMAN'S DAUGHTERS IV
THE BOSS MAN'S DAUGHTERS **V**
A SAVAGE LOVE **I & II**
BAE BELONGS TO ME
A HUSTLER'S DECEIT I, II, III
WHAT BAD BITCHES DO I, II
By **Aryanna**
A KINGPIN'S AMBITON

176

A KINGPIN'S AMBITION **II**

I MURDER FOR THE DOUGH

By **Ambitious**

TRUE SAVAGE

TRUE SAVAGE II

TRUE SAVAGE **III**

TRUE SAVAGE **IV**

TRUE SAVAGE **V**

TRUE SAVAGE **VI**

By **Chris Green**

A DOPEBOY'S PRAYER

By **Eddie "Wolf" Lee**

THE KING CARTEL **I, II & III**

By **Frank Gresham**

THESE NIGGAS AIN'T LOYAL **I, II & III**

By **Nikki Tee**

GANGSTA SHYT **I II &III**

By **CATO**

THE ULTIMATE BETRAYAL

By **Phoenix**

BOSS'N UP **I , II & III**

By **Royal Nicole**

I LOVE YOU TO DEATH

By Destiny J

I RIDE FOR MY HITTA

I STILL RIDE FOR MY HITTA

By **Misty Holt**

LOVE & CHASIN' PAPER

By **Qay Crockett**

TO DIE IN VAIN

SINS OF A HUSTLA

By **ASAD**

BROOKLYN HUSTLAZ

By **Boogsy Morina**

BROOKLYN ON LOCK I & II

By **Sonovia**

GANGSTA CITY

By **Teddy Duke**

A DRUG KING AND HIS DIAMOND I & II III

A DOPEMAN'S RICHES

HER MAN, MINE'S TOO I, II

CASH MONEY HO'S

By Nicole Goosby

TRAPHOUSE KING **I II & III**

KINGPIN KILLAZ I II III

STREET KINGS

By **Hood Rich**

LIPSTICK KILLAH **I, II**

CRIME OF PASSION I & II

By **Mimi**

STEADY MOBBN' **I, II**

By **Marcellus Allen**

WHO SHOT YA **I, II**

Renta

GORILLAZ IN THE BAY **I II**

DE'KARI

TRIGGADALE

Elijah R. Freeman

GOD BLESS THE TRAPPERS I, II, III

THESE SCANDALOUS STREETS I, II, III

FEAR MY GANGSTA I, II, III

THESE STREETS DON'T LOVE NOBODY I, II

BURY ME A G I, II, III, IV, V

A GANGSTA'S EMPIRE I, II, III

Tranay Adams

THE STREETS ARE CALLING

Duquie Wilson

MARRIED TO A BOSS…

By Destiny Skai & Chris Green

KINGS OF THE GAME II

Playa Ray

BOOKS BY LDP'S CEO, CA$H

TRUST IN NO MAN

TRUST IN NO MAN 2

TRUST IN NO MAN 3

BONDED BY BLOOD

SHORTY GOT A THUG

THUGS CRY

THUGS CRY 2

THUGS CRY 3

TRUST NO BITCH

TRUST NO BITCH 2

TRUST NO BITCH 3

TIL MY CASKET DROPS

RESTRAINING ORDER

RESTRAINING ORDER 2

IN LOVE WITH A CONVICT

Coming Soon

BONDED BY BLOOD 2

BOW DOWN TO MY GANGSTA

Kingpin Killaz 3